THE D.  PAY

A DCI GARRICK ѠILLER - BOOK 6

M.G. COLE

TANGLEBOX
BOOKS

THE DEAD DON'T PAY
A DCI Garrick mystery - Book 6

Copyright © 2022 by Max Cole (M.G.Cole)

Cover art: Shutterstock

THE DEAD DON'T PAY

1

Relentless rain had churned the sloping ground into slick mud. No, it was more than mud, Addison thought. It was a treacherous paste that seeped into the most resilient boot and pull a man to his death.

That would be a fitting demise for one who had committed the direst of acts. But not a fate that Addison was willing to contemplate. At least, not for him. He glanced back at his companion who stumbled over a gnarled tree root that carpeted the forest floor and only appeared when the beam of their head torches swept across them.

The wet canvas in his hands slipped through his fingers. The additional weight of water made the already heavy package almost impossible to carry up the hill. At the other end of the six-foot rolled sheet, Liam Brady grunted in effort, his asthmatic breathing worsening with each exhausted step as the damp settled on his chest. Addison was convinced his partner in crime wasn't bearing his half of the weight as the canvas slapped against the rocks and mud of the hill beneath.

"Watch it!" Addison growled for the umpteenth time since they'd left the van. Brady's retort was lost in a howl of wind and the increased tattoo of rain against Addison's hooded jacket. The package's value was incalculable and as of this moment both their fates rested with it.

He was so preoccupied glowering at Brady that he stumbled on a rock in the darkness. His ankle gave a sharp jerk to the side. If he hadn't been wearing sensible Salomon boots, then he was sure his ankle would have been twisted, or worse. A puddle splashed his jeans and ran down into his socks, adding to the freezing water accumulating in the sole. The venomous curse he screamed was lost in the storm.

It would be worth it, he assured himself. An hour from now, he'd be back home. Melting in a warm shower, then he'd be ready to start jump back into the *search*. It was that another critical part of his future. Completing that puzzle was the key to *everything*.

He just had to stay alive long enough to do so.

Brady's whining voice rose from behind. "How much further?"

The last couple of months had been a real test of patience for Addison. As the plan fermented and the opportunities became clear, he'd further committed to their mission. The only weak link was Brady. Without him, none of this would have happened. But with him, the months had been intolerable.

The canvas was sharply yanked again as Brady slowed down. Addison's fingers were so numb that it was almost torn from his hand. Dropping the package now could be a disaster.

"Keep movin', you arsehole!" he yelled back, his eyes scanning the gloom ahead. He recognised nothing. It was just shy of a full moon tonight, which would've provided just enough light to navigate the peak, but a week of foul weather had built to a storm that had flooded large portions of the county.

Brady's grumbling continued, but Addison tuned it out as they abruptly stepped from the forest into a clearing. Luckily, they hadn't strayed off course. A large moss-covered boulder sat off-centre, half-poking from the earth.

"Can't believe we made it," he chuckled darkly. "Come on."

With a grunt, he gave a final haul on the canvas sheet as they carefully laid it in front of the rock. Addison sat on the boulder to catch his breath. His jeans were sodden, so the cold wet seat was a relief, not a discomfort.

"Beats the heat," Brady said without a trace of irony.

Addison used his sleeve to wipe the rain from his eyes. As far as he was concerned, the money he'd soon make would ensure he spent the rest of his life somewhere warm and luxurious.

Liam Brady crouched and partially opened the canvass sheet. A shovel lay on top of a wooden crate that was already split open from several impacts on the ground. The hay they'd used for packing was now spilling out. He stood straight with a sigh and used his toes to nudge the packing material back inside. Then he struck the tip of the shovel into the waterlogged earth.

"Are you gonna give me a hand?"

Addison nodded but didn't move. "Give me a minute. I'm knackered."

"The sooner we start the sooner we can leave." Brady hacked at the waterlogged ground. The dirt easily came out in large scoops. "Why didn't you bring two of these bloody things?" He shook the spade for emphasis.

Addison didn't want to admit that was an oversight neither man had thought of. Every option had been thoroughly stress-tested – or so he thought. What else had they overlooked? For the next few squelching spadefuls of earth, Addison felt his resolve wavering. Was there something glaring, right in front of them, that would upturn their plan? Something so obvious that the police would be on them the moment he arrived home?

No. Don't think like that, he warned himself. He'd been meticulous. He cast the negative words aside. A shovel is one thing, but the integral plan was watertight. Liam Brady was the only weak point, and he had a backup just in case.

They were beyond the point of no return. There were too many serious players who wouldn't blink to see either man dead. In the beam of his head torch, he watched Brady cast heaps of earth out into the darkness. "Watch what you're doing, dickhead! Don't toss the dirt back down the hill. We need it to fill in the bloody hole!"

With a sharp huff, Brady speared the shovel into the dirt, deep enough for it to stand freely.

"I know what I'm doing."

Irritated, Addison shoved Brady aside and snatched the spade from his hand. With all his strength, he speared the tip of the blade into the soft earth, powering it down with his boot. The mud gave a sucking wet sound as he levered a large clod out and carefully tipped it a yard away. He piled it neatly to the side. He stabbed the dirt again and again with mounting anger as he rapidly carved a hole deep enough to conceal the evidence. But it was still not long enough. Exhausted, he thrust the spade back into Brady's hand, knocking the vape from his colleague's hand. He'd produced it from his jacket and had been quietly sucking on as Addison did all the graft. It was a welcome change to the chain-smoking Brady usually did. The man was a pig.

"You idiot!" Brady barked, crouching to retrieve it. "That was brand new!"

"You'll be able to buy as many as you want soon enough. Finish the hole."

Brady caught the dull red LED on the vape and picked it up.

"Uh! Look, it's cracked. It's leaking everywhere..."

"I don't care! It's your turn!"

Once again, Addison sat on the boulder to recover and tune out his companion's complaints. Each word grated his nerves. Prior to the accident, everything had been plain sailing. Since then, they'd been looking over their shoulders at every turn.

To his credit, Brady quickly widened the hole, and soon excavated a knee-deep rectangle. Stones clanged off the sharp blade with increasing frequency as he dug deeper.

Addison traced the light over Brady's face. His expression was set in such deep concentration, he didn't notice the light playing across him. Water dripped from his Roman nose in an almost constant torrent. He seemed to take his fury out on the planet beneath his feet.

"That's enough." Brady stopped digging and looked up, wincing as he was blinded by the light. He held up his hand to shadow it. "You're blinding me, you pillock!"

Addison moved to the end of the canvas wrap. Brady silently took the other, and they both shuffled to the edge of the hole. Both men ached from the physical labour, but still ensured they gently lowered the canvas into the hole.

It was deep enough, thought Addison with relief. More than deep enough...

Brady took the shovel and motioned to fill the hole in.

"I'll do it," Addison snapped and reached for the spade.

As if second-guessing his intentions, Brady didn't relinquish his grip and held fast. Both men were suddenly locked into a shoving match. Addison's skull rattled as Brady head-butted him – breaking both head torches in the process and plunging the scene into darkness. Now they had to rely on their senses as they wrestled for control of the spade.

A knee to the groin forced one man to let go. It was a fatal mistake.

With a gelatinous squelch, the blade punctured through fabric and into a chest cavity. Ribs cracked as the shaft was violently twisted. Wet flesh tore. And the victim's screams were silenced as their lungs were punctured.

There was no let-up in the savage attack, fuelled by pent-up hatred. The shovel blade was pulled free. A quick spin around brought the blade clean across the injured man's throat – beheading him. The head dropped into the shallow grave, followed by the body expelling five litres of blood across the canvas sack.

2

_____

"It's been a while," Molly Meyers said as she gently drummed her fingers at the side of her Costa Coffee mug. Her perfectly manicured nails were painted a vivid red, and she was conscious enough to crook the fingers of her left hand, so it wasn't too obvious that the pinkie was missing.

The gentle rattle of her nails against the rim of the mug distracted DCI David Garrick just enough to derail his own thoughts.

"Mmm?" he drew his gaze back to her wide jade eyes and charming freckled smile that was steadily gaining her more avid viewers and online fans as her popularity rose. Starting as journalist for a local rag, her career had been catapulted when she followed Garrick's adventures. He had a knack of being embroiled in high-profile stories that made the national news. It had rapidly landed her a regional spot at the BBC as a TV reporter. Shortly after that, she became the news when she was kidnapped. It was an event from which she still carried heavy mental scars, but her external persona revealed none of the angst beneath. It had pushed her career that extra step forward, propelling her onto national TV spots. Her eloquent ability to deliver emotional heavy stories with a human touch, coupled with her natural camera-friendly looks, had assisted her ascent.

"You're here, but your mind has left the building." Molly's eyes never left him as she sipped her mocha.

Garrick poured in a second sachet of sugar and stirred his green tea. "You know how it is. Work and life are not always compatible bed fellows."

"Tough case?"

"Less so than usual."

The fact was that he and his team had been entrenched in more paperwork than crime solving. Kent's major criminals seemed to have fallen silent over the last couple of months, replaced by mundane incidents any old detective could solve in their sleep.

"I've got a new Guv," Garrick added as he sipped his tea.

"Ah, I heard Drury had left. Well, was *forced* to move on is what I heard."

Garrick shrugged. "I'm not privy to the lofty workings of senior management. And I can't be bothered listening to gossip."

"It sounds as if life's more boring than stressful."

Garrick chuckled. "Why can't it be both?"

Molly watched as he emptied another two sugar sleeves into his tea. He caught her look.

"What?"

"You've developed a sweet tooth since I last saw you."

"Are you monitoring my health?"

Molly smiled and shrugged nonchalantly, although Garrick knew better. Her powers of observation were exceptional, and she's probably mentally filed all his habits away from the first couple of times they'd met. He'd once told her she'd make a superb detective, and he meant it.

"And Wendy's pregnant." He blurted the words out without thinking. Molly's eyes widened a little, giving him the vindication that she didn't know *everything*. Although now she did. He wasn't sure why he had told her. Outside his work colleagues, he didn't have a circle of friends and had no family to confide in. Even Lord, Wilkes, Fanta, and Chib were unaware of his pending parental responsibilities, although he was convinced Fanta had somehow worked it out.

"Wow. Congratulations. How far along is she?"

"Nearly three months."

Wendy had already started talking to him in units of *weeks*, which was something he struggled to convert. He was old-school and had no intention of changing. That was the main reason he hadn't had time to meet up with Molly. As soon as he'd found out that he was going to be a father, a maelstrom of questions had consumed his attention.

The most shameful of which had been whether he'd *wanted* to be a father.

It was against his character to accept that he had no choice. Of course he did. Or at least he *thought* he did. He loved Wendy; he had no doubts about that. But raising a child at his age... was it practical? It also meant he and Wendy had better forge a strong future together – just as she'd quit her job as a teaching assistant to pursue a new career. A move that had just lost her paid maternity cover, meaning that the burden of supporting all three of them now crushed his shoulders and his chest. He suddenly became aware Molly had asked him a question. She read his expression and repeated.

"Too early to tell the make?" His confused look made her smile. "Boy or girl?"

"Not yet, no. We're still deciding whether we should know." That was a fabrication. Wendy was undecided. He was desperate to know. After all, he was a detective. Hoovering up information was second nature to him.

"Congratulations, anyway." Molly clinked her mug against his glass. "Perhaps this isn't the best time to pick your brain."

Garrick sniggered at the comment. After removing the growth that had been applying pressure on his brain, it was the flippant comment he used around the station to telegraph he was fine with people knowing. Again, that wasn't quite true, but such were the little lies that made living with others possible.

He tapped the side of his head where the scar was still healing. Hair had started to conceal it, but it still made him self-conscious.

"I have a hole right here you can pick away at."

Molly gave a polite chuckle, but it was clearly forced. She sipped her coffee again and put the cup down before continuing.

"It's about your sister."

Garrick nodded. Molly had originally told him she wanted to discuss it months ago. Emilie was the victim of a diabolical organised Murder Club, led by his close friend at the time, John Howard. She and her fiancé had been killed in Illinois, USA, but her body had never been found. Since then, the perverse members of this exclusive club had used this as a psychological weapon against Garrick, in an elaborate scheme that John Howard had conjured from the grave. The club's tendrils reached internationally and had caused

Molly's kidnapping and the subsequent removal of Superintendent Margery Drury. It was a prime story for any reporter, but since Molly had found herself in the heart of it, he could hardly ask her to stop poking around, no matter how raw his emotions still were. Garrick nodded for her to continue.

"Because of what happened," she circled a finger between the two of them to concisely encapsulate the whole kidnapping incident, "the case has hit the press more than it did when Emilie and Sam McKinzie were killed." Naturally, Garrick's own cases had brought the subject back into the spotlight, but he had ignored most of it. And as is ever the case with news cycles, world events quickly overtook the story. "And still the facts are wishy-washy, and there's never been a real focus on what happened out there."

"DCI Kane is still investigating that at the Met." Kane had once placed Garrick under suspicion, even planting Chib as an agent within his team. An act Garrick had come to terms with, even if some members of the team hadn't. "I'm sure he'll have something to say about nosing around."

Molly gave an innocent shrug. "Then he should work faster. Plus, it's not up to him. The FBI is leading the investigation. Which makes this a bigger story."

Garrick nodded in agreement. If it wasn't for Molly's personal involvement, then he would've guessed that she had her sights on an international audience. He acknowledged that was a sceptical thought. But that was his nature.

"You know what I know." He took a long gulp of the sweet green tea. It lubricated his suddenly dry throat. He hadn't spoken about his sister for months, and as the Murder Club case had shifted over to Kane's team, he had no more involvement.

"That's my point. Nobody knows anything. We're both personally wrapped up in this. You more than anybody–"

Garrick waved a finger. "I'll stop you there. I told you before, I'm not speaking about this on camera."

She answered him with a sly smile. "Detective, it's not your charming vox pop I want on camera. I'd rather you be behind it." Garrick's deepening frown made her chuckle again. "I'm putting together an investigational documentary about the Murder Club, and it's going to focus on the one missing piece."

"Emilie."

"She's the heart of the story. A story that needs to be told. For her."

Garrick didn't know what to say.

Molly shifted in her chair, a slight betrayal of how awkward she felt. "The BBC looks as if they are going to green light it. I'll have a small production team and we'll shoot Stateside and follow her trail. I'd like you to come with me."

A tingle rushed through Garrick. In the early days, he'd courted the idea of going over the pond and banging heads at the Flora Police Department who were originally handling the case. That was until a car with DNA of Emelie and another victim were found across the Stateline in New York, triggering FBI involvement. Ultimately, his professionalism had taken charge, and he assured himself that the American cops were doing their jobs with due diligence.

However, the offer to go over and see the crime scene himself was almost too tempting to refuse. It was also irresponsible. Wendy needed him here and his new Super was a man devoid of charisma, who appeared to think Garrick's successful record was nothing short of him showing off, rather than a job well done.

"When?"

Molly indecisively moved her head side-to-side, her wavy bobbed red hair danced across her face. "Next month, perhaps. Once we get a green light, I need a budget, a fixer in the States... but we'll be able to go. Ask the questions that need asking. And ask the ones that haven't been."

Garrick leaned back in his seat and the two stared at one another in companionable silence, one hewn from mutual suffering and understanding. Molly arched a perfect eyebrow.

"Tempting, isn't it?"

Garrick's silence was saved by his phone buzzing. It was a text message from Chib. With a deep sigh, he knocked back the rest of his tea. He stood.

"Let me think about it."

Molly nodded at the phone in his hand. "Then out of courtesy I won't ask what's so pressing."

"Just the usual," he said with a cryptic smile. "Thanks for the tea."

Garrick hurried from the Costa, thankful that he may finally have something more demanding to take up his time.

3

"I was looking for a change of pace, Chib. But this isn't quite what I had in mind."

Garrick's nostrils flared as the pervasive smell assaulted him. He looked forlornly around the sprawling rubbish tip. He and Detective Sergeant Chibarameze Okon stood atop a twelve-foot pile of household waste like a pair of armchair mountaineers. Rain pattered from the hood of his Barbour jacket, keeping his head dry but forming a funnel that channelled the stench of the dump directly into his face. He couldn't stop heaving and hoped the egg sandwich he'd had for lunch didn't threaten to return.

"Slow day," said Chib. She had the sense to wear a paper mask across her mouth and nose which went someway to easing the nasal assault.

"Slow month," Garrick mumbled as they stared at the rubbish.

Staff at the Hermitage Quarry Recycling Centre had been vigilant enough to spot something suspicious in a recent trash deposit. No mean feat when anything untoward was so easily concealed in tons of household waste. An item was easily lost when it was loaded into a bin wagon, merging with an entire neighbourhood's rubbish before being tipped into a pile of month-old trash and bulldozed together. This was a place entire bodies could vanish without a trace. Despite this, staff were trained to keep an eye out for the smallest of oddities.

Garrick crouched, positioning him closer to the ripe fermenting smell rising from the ground, but it gave him a better view of the shovel that had risen from the waste like Excalibur as the piles had been churned. The blade and lower shaft were covered in dried blood. In the grey daylight, it was difficult to tell where the crusted blood ended and where it replaced ground-in dirt, but it was clear enough for Garrick to tell it was a *lot* of blood.

Chib pointed to a ripped bag close by. It too was stained with blood that partially obscured the *bag for life* logo.

"I reckon it was originally wrapped in that. The blade, at least. Then dropped in a wheelie bin."

Garrick looked between the two objects. It was certainly suspicious, but there could be a rational explanation. Until it was analysed, it could even just be red paint.

"The tip of the shovel handle has been cut to fit in the wheelie bin." Garrick pointed out. He gave the ground one last curious look but couldn't see anything else amiss. He stood with the accompanying sound of his knees clicking. "We'll drop it into forensics and see what we've got."

With gloved hands, Chib carefully picked up the shovel and bag for life. They stumbled back down the incline. Damp waste moved underfoot, threatening to trip them. Garrick was sure the smell was now ingrained in his clothes. They would need incinerating but chucking them straight into the washing machine would have do once he returned home. At the bottom of the mound, they headed towards the Portakabins that formed the site office. The staff were waiting inside until the police had concluded their business before they could resume work. As it was already late afternoon, Garrick suspected they'd all be sent home early.

He wished he could leave early too, but he had to return to the station for the last few hours of tedious paperwork.

IT WAS close to eleven o'clock and Wendy still hadn't returned from her friends. Since discovering that she was pregnant, she'd spent more time with Sonia, a taciturn redhead from their hiking group. Garrick had met her half a dozen times and spectacularly failed to strike up a conversation or even a smile from the woman. He was surprised somebody as gregarious as Wendy had struck up a friendship with her. She kept the group's blog up to date and he had the vague recollection that she worked for the ferries or something. But at least it gave Wendy company when he wasn't around.

He sat on the sofa in front of the TV playing a repeat of *Have I Got News For You*, as he carefully read through a letter from the conveyancer he'd instructed to deal with the sale of his house. He'd accepted the first decent offer on the property. Ever mindful of his percentage, the estate agent tried to convince him to hold out for a lot more, but after the brutal killing that had taken place there, Garrick would've happily taken a financial hit just to get it off his hands. Still, the first offer more than covered his outstanding mortgage and left him with a handsome profit that would've been enough to get them a slightly bigger home together rather than stay in their current small rental.

But that had been before Wendy had quit her job and then announced they had a baby on the way. In an ideal world, they would have moved into his house, which had been large enough for the three of them, but the world was far from ideal.

As far as he could tell, the deal seemed in order after a surveyor's assessment. As he didn't need the sale to move on, and it was a first-time buyer, there was no endless property chain to trap him. All that was required was his signature and the deal would be swiftly concluded.

Yet his biro hovered over the signature line as his thoughts drifted to Molly Meyers' offer.

The opportunity to go to America and trace the path of his sister. The chance to finally put the horrors to bed and move on with his life.

Or was he chasing ghosts?

The last few months had seen John Howard's insidious club unravel and loose ends tied up. Gradually, the chain that had been around his neck had slackened. Not finding his sister's body was an emotional barb that would forever sting, but as a professional copper, he had to accept that sometimes victims were never found.

He reminded himself to focus on the positives.

His tumour had been successfully removed and his private consultant, Doctor Rajasekar, was pleased with his recovery. While he still had the occasional wobble, the odd whispering murmur in the darkness, or slight flutter of mental confusion, it was nothing that would have him removed off the force. His career was doing very well, and he now had a growing family.

He starred at the fossil on the mantelpiece. The only one of his collection that he'd unpacked since moving in with Wendy. It was the last one he had started to clean, yet it was still unfinished and cracked from his previous efforts. He hated that it represented his old life. Frozen in time.

Garrick swished his signature across the contract just as he heard the front door open, and Wendy announce herself.

For the first time in his life, he had everything he need.

A WEEK of relative tranquillity peaked when Chib handed out invites to her wedding. It triggered Fanta to dash from the station and organise a doughnut and soda celebration. The weekend was tinged with an odd feeling of foreboding when he told Wendy about the invite.

"I'm now a plus-one?" she said, turning the silver-foiled invitation in her fingers.

Garrick slowly coasted an electric toothbrush over his molars, so grunted positively.

"What's her other half like?"

"Dunno," he said, trying not to spit toothpaste everywhere. "She's very priv-it..."

"Privit?"

"Pri-vate!" he indicated the toothbrush.

Wendy giggled. "For a detective, you don't ask a lot of questions."

Garrick walked into the bathroom and spat the foam from his mouth, rinsed with mouthwash, then headed back into the bedroom. Wendy was looking dreamily at the invitation.

"We have a good team environment because nobody asks questions," Garrick said, slipping on an old Hard Rock Cafe t-shirt an ex had once got him from Vegas, which now served as faded pyjamas when the nights got chilly.

"So you don't talk about us?"

"I'm the boss. Of course I don't."

"That's a million miles from how it used to be at my school."

A sixth sense warned Garrick he was steering towards conversational rocks. He climbed into bed and quickly changed the subject.

"The conveyancer emailed today. We should exchange by Friday." He'd expected a bigger reaction than the half smile playing at the corner of Wendy's mouth. "Are you feeling alright?"

"Fine. I was just thinking..." She rolled to face him and playfully tapped the invitation on Garrick's chest. "She's Nigerian, right?" Garrick nodded. "Will it be a Nigerian wedding? That sounds so epic."

"I don't know. I don't think she gets on with her family." He tried to recall past conversations with Chib. "I don't even know if they approve of the wedding."

"You'll have to ask."

"If I dare."

"They must be in love if they're young and still willing to make things formal."

"I suppose..." Once again, Garrick felt that he was approaching a danger zone he'd rather avoid. He reached for the Clive Cussler novel on his bedside table that had remained on the same page for the last four months. As he slowly flicked through to the old lottery ticket that served as a bookmark, he heard Wendy sigh and roll over to turn her bedside light off.

For some reason that Garrick couldn't put his finger on,

the talk of marriage made him feel uncomfortable, taking the shine off the good feeling he'd been enjoying lately. Wendy fell quickly asleep without another word. Nothing more was mentioned about Chib or weddings, yet, for the first time since he could remember, a tense atmosphere swaddled the weekend.

Garrick was relieved to sit at his desk Monday morning and read the forensic report about the shovel. It was human blood.

And they had identified the owner.

4

From the state of the end terrace house's front garden, the shovel certainly hadn't been used at this property, at least for its intended purpose. The B-negative blood had DNA flagged up on the NDNAD – the National DNA Database, from Liam Brady's arrest some twelve years ago. It was an altercation in university and no charges were filed, but the DNA profile remained on the system.

Garrick rang the doorbell but didn't expect any response. The windows had a thin layer of grime and the net curtains beyond were stained nicotine yellow. The house was a rental property and was the current registered address of the man they were looking for.

Chib had remained behind at the station to sort through outstanding paperwork for the Crown Prosecution Service's request from their last big arson case, although Garrick suspected that she was using the time to arrange her wedding. Nobody had been keen on coming with him to chase what they all considered would amount to a non-case.

It was even an effort to coax Fanta to step out into the chill autumn day. She'd constantly asked for more fieldwork experience, but after a series of recent rough and traumatic cases, he wondered if she'd had her fill. Was the once-keen Detective Constable having doubts about her career path? Garrick hoped not. Her ability for sniffing out leads was exactly what the force desperately needed. By the second press of the doorbell, she was already on her phone.

"What're you doing?"

"Calling a locksmith. If anybody's home, I think they might be lying in a pool of the rest of that blood."

He agreed, pleased with her fluid assessment. Already on the drive to Sittingbourne she'd looked up the bin pickup days, identified the council team making the rounds the day the shovel would've been chucked away. That was an easy guess as bin collections were fortnightly. It was still an enormous amount of time and resources for a bloodied shovel. Nevertheless, they had a duty of care to investigate the merest *whiff* of a crime. The locksmith would appear as a line on his department's budget, which he would have to defend when the new Gov inevitably challenged it. Garrick was of the growing opinion that the biggest waste of police resources was middle-management, but he wasn't stupid enough to voice that out loud.

They passed the time waiting for the locksmith, sitting in Fanta's car, and discussing idle chit-chat. From her subtle steering of the conversation, he could tell she'd caught wind of Wendy's pregnancy and wanted to ask more. She was also prudent enough not to directly ask him. How she'd found out, Garrick couldn't fathom. He was sure he'd been silent on the matter. He'd only told Drury after she'd left her position, and that had been in the wilds of the golf links. And if Fanta knew, then his whole team would be ablaze with gossip. In retrospect, some of his answers were so vague as to sound evasive enough to confirm her suspicions. He was relieved when her passive aggressive interrogation ended with the arrival of the locksmith. He slipped a thin metal plate between the door jamb, where the Yale lock sat and rammed it back and forth a few times was enough to force the door open. The basic skill took minutes to master and had just pocketed the man almost two-hundred quid.

The stale smell from the hallway struck both Garrick and Fanta as they stepped inside the dark hallway. The 1920s build provided little external light, so the entrance and stair-case were shrouded in darkness. The corridor ended at the rear of the property, in a small kitchen. A door to the gable-end took them into the living room.

"Hello? Police!" Garrick shouted. Only the soft murmur of traffic outside answered him.

"What a dump," breathed Fanta.

There was a threadbare sofa that would look more at home in a landfill, and a small wooden coffee table with over-lapping cup-stains burned through to the veneer. A cheap TV stood in the corner, balanced on another old table. The screen was smudged with fingerprints and dust. The plastic casing cracked. Other than a grime-covered gas fire and a bare lightbulb, there was nothing else. The nicotine smell was ingrained, but Garrick saw no sign of an ashtray.

"How long had he rented the property?"

"Thirteen months. So he had time to turn it into a home."

The kitchen was similarly spartan, with a dirty gas oven and hob. A smattering of utensils were in a metal holder on the draining board. Three plates, a single bowl, and a cracked white mug with a faded building company logo on it. A jar of instant Nescafe sat next to a dirty spoon. The coffee granules had congealed together.

"Cornflakes and... some dodgy strawberry jam." Fanta angled the jar in the weak light filtering through the mottled window. "Complete with its own fungal growth. Gross." She opened the other cupboards, then finally the small yellowing refrigerator. The light didn't come one, and there wasn't the faintest chilly breeze. "Power's off. And he's left is a carton of cheese. Well, it used to be milk." She gagged at the smell and slammed the door closed. "I'd say all this crap is weeks old."

"The bin collection is every fortnight." Garrick used his foot to flick open the tarnished peddle bin in the corner. It was empty. "So somebody was here at least two and a half weeks ago."

They retraced their steps and went upstairs. The wooden floorboards were visible through holes in the threadbare dark red carpet and they creaked alarmingly as they ascended. Fanta led the way, but he noticed she was hesitating. Her assured attitude had frosted over. The last time the two of them had entered an empty house and walked upstairs, she had almost died.

"Are you okay?"

"Sure. Why?" She replied too quickly.

Garrick didn't see the point in pressing her. The last few stairs turned right at the top, ending at a small landing. The bathroom door was open directly ahead of them, a hideous avocado suite on display. Worn lino clung to the floor in patches. The sink and bath were stained with scum marks. The toilet lid was open, its contents dark brown and indescribable.

"The guy's worse than a pig!" Fanta said, rapidly backing out.

The next door was an airing cupboard. Garrick touched the boiler tank. "Cold."

Another closed door took them into an empty room overlooking the backyard, which was little more than a few square feet of concrete with weeds pushing through the cracks. That left the bedroom overlooking the main road.

The door opened with a dry creak. The curtains were open, filtered by more nets shaded with nicotine blotches. A single bed, with some grubby sheets, was left unmade in the corner. A well-used plastic suitcase spilled clothes to the floor. All of them worn, the underwear skid mark hell. A bedside table held an empty Pilsner bottle and an ashtray overflowing with cigarette butts. But it was the wall that grabbed their attention.

The peeling brown wallpaper was almost covered in handwritten notes, maps with locations circled and arrows pointing in obscure directions. Curious, they moved closer. Fanta tried the light switch, but there was no power. She used the flashlight on her mobile phone to shed light on a printout. It was a list of books bought from Amazon.

"I think we have a serial librarian." She frowned as she moved over to a map. It was an ordinance survey map of the countryside. It had been enlarged, and there were no place names to aid orientation. A red line had been drawn along it, following the contours of the landscape. Other coloured lines - blue squares, green triangles - were peppered across other similar maps. A general map of Kent had a X marked close to the coast. A more detailed road map had an A-road highlighted in front of a lone house, but the road name was missing.

Fanta started taking pictures of wall. "It's the ramblings of a mad man."

Garrick took it all in. "Or maybe it is." He took a step back to take in the whole ensemble. "Or... this might sound bonkers, but we may be looking at a treasure map..."

5

"It's difficult to investigate a crime, when one hasn't happened," said Garrick without taking his eyes off his computer screen. He wasn't the fastest typist, and sorting through his emails was always at the bottom of his priority list. But with the downtime offered between cases, it was a chance to work through the four-hundred and twenty-six messages clogging his mailbox. "That's probably the first rule of police work," he corrected himself.

From two desks away, he heard Fanta huff in annoyance. Two days had passed since they'd visited the house and DC Fanta Liu hadn't stopped talking about it.

"The tenant still hasn't returned," she pointed out.

"Have you been stalking him? Now that is a crime."

DC Sean Wilkes's sniggering carried across the quiet office. He and Fanta had been dating for a while now and Garrick suspected they'd moved in together, although nothing had been officially announced. To their credit, the young detectives kept their personal life out of the police station. For the most part, anyway.

"I've knocked at the house twice since," she replied tartly. "And spoke to the neighbours. He hasn't been seen for almost a month."

"I never used to see my neighbours for months at a time," said Garrick. "People have busy lives. He could be on holiday. Or visiting friends. Or even living somewhere else. None of which is a crime."

"He is a missing person!"

"I'm sure he knows where he is." Garrick heard another splutter of laughter from Wilkes and predicted trouble ahead for him. "Look at it this way. The blood on the shovel matched Brady. But he could've had a gardening accident and bled all over the thing without dying." Fanta wasn't happy with that excuse. Garrick pressed on. "And *he* lived there. Somebody from that house put the shovel in the recycling bin. The logical person would be Liam Brady himself. And since nobody has reported him missing…"

"Oh, so you have to be reported missing before anybody cares? What about people who live alone?"

Garrick looked up. Fanta was giving him a hard stare. She was the most socially sensitive member of the team. Whether that came from her Chinese heritage that promoted strong community ties, or was a quirk of her generation, or a little of both, he couldn't tell. But social injustice always triggered her.

Garrick shrugged. "That's the way life is. We're not talking about whether it's fair." He could see she was about to speak again. "And it wouldn't be fair if we're accused of wasting resources chasing non-cases amid budget cuts."

The warning was enough. Fanta slouched in her chair and returned to the incident file she was preparing to send to the CPS. Intricate paperwork went hand-in-hand with every case. Some rare officers enjoyed the tedium, but Fanta expressed her displeasure in a series of grumbles that carried across the loudest office.

"The NFS is a relic," she muttered, referring to the National File Service framework she had to deliver evidence in. She was irked that some cases were well over a year old by the time they went to prosecution, and the details had long shunted out of her short attention span. The proposed budget cuts threatened to increase the admin. A nightmare for any jobbing detective.

"DC Liu, today may be your lucky day," said Garrick, reading a report on his screen.

"Why? Has somebody died?" Fanta muttered under her breath.

"Yes. Horribly."

GARRICK WHISTLED as Chib pulled through a pair of stately iron gates. "Now, *that's* a house!"

The Nissan Leaf rattled over a cattle grid. The metallic rumble was amplified because of the electric car's near-silence. It set Garrick's teeth on edge. The house ahead was a huge modern construction that belonged to an extravagant episode of *Grand Designs*. Dark titanium panels branched from the structure at obtuse angles, while pure white marble peeked through geometric gaps. Poised against the mani-cured lawn, it was supposed to be a vision of the future, but right now it was a crime scene. Six police vehicles were parked outside, next to a black panel van with *Spitfire Security* emblazon on the side. Officers looked up expectantly as Chib parked the car. A young Indian woman approached Garrick with a nod of recognition.

"Afternoon, sir."

She looked familiar and Garrick racked his brain for a name, but it didn't come. "What do we have here?"

"Homeowner, a Mrs Kirsty Flanagan. The intruder alarm was activated at lunchtime." She nodded towards the Spitfire van. "By the time the patrol arrived to investigate, he found her dead in the kitchen."

She led Garrick and Chib through the open front door and into a spacious hall that stretched two stories high and was capped by an elaborate glass dome that flooded the entrance with natural light. A staircase spiralled to the next floor, with framed paintings of ancient buildings. Garrick recognised a few: Petra, the Parthenon, and the Acropolis. The kitchen was through a short corridor to the left. The blinding-white ceramic floor and cabinets, topped by black stone countertops, complimented the house well - if it wasn't for the copious splattering of blood everywhere. There was so much that Chib stopped short. Garrick heard a sharp intake of breath from the uniformed officer next to him. She looked uneasy seeing such savagery on display. The air was sharp with the distinctive smell of blood, so much that he could almost taste it.

Kirsty Flanagan was sprawled across the tiled floor on her front, which was a blessing, as they couldn't see her face. Or what was left of it. The back of her skull had been struck so hard that it had flattened in places to no wider than her palm. The raw gaping wound revealed jagged white shards of broken skull and brain matter. Blood had sprayed every-where, spilling across the floor, and leaving a trail of foot-prints that led to an open patio door with a view of the cultivated back garden. A bloodied sledged hammer, the sort used in roadside construction, had been tossed into the corner of the room.

Careful not to step in the blood, Garrick slowly walked around the victim. Chib and the officer stayed at the door, their grimaces of horror unchanged.

"Is SOCO on their way?"

Chib nodded and took a phone from her jacket pocket. "I'll get an ETA."

Garrick looked between the open patio, the hammer, and the victim. "The killer didn't try to hide their tracks." He crouched at the body, unable to stop a gasp of effort from escaping his lips. "My guess is a strike from behind put her down." He indicated to the mashed head. "And then the attacker repeatedly struck her. I reckon that she'd be dead from the first blow. This is something more passionate or animalistic." He spotted a knife on the counter. It was in a wooden block that would have been within the victim's reach before she fell. Then he looked at the sledgehammer. "That's hardly a discreet weapon to bring to a murder."

Chib hung up the phone and carefully walked around the crime scene until she was at the open patio door.

"This doesn't appear to be forced. Maybe it was already unlocked?" She glanced at the windows. "They're all shut."

"The security guy didn't see any initial signs of a break in," the officer said, breathing heavily to compose herself. "He said he'd checked around the property until he found the door open."

"Any signs of other vehicles?"

"No, but her car doesn't appear to be here."

"Put it out as stolen." Garrick knew it could be in a garage, borrowed, or any other number of excuses, but with the murder relatively fresh, there was no time to second-guess. "Family?"

"According to the security guy, she's a widow."

Garrick was impressed with the questions the officer had already asked, considering such a gruesome crime scene.

"Did he know her well?"

The officer shook her head. "He said she was nice enough, but very paranoid."

"About what?"

The officer shrugged. "With all this security, probably about getting robbed."

"There's a small TV over there." Garrick pointed to the corner of the kitchen. "An opportunistic thief would've taken what they could." He indicated her left hand. "And she still has a ring." A white gold band glinted in the rapidly deterio-rating light.

Kirsty's blonde, blood-matted hair obscured her face, and Garrick wondered how old she was. She wore black jogging pants and a matching top that was unzipped and open as it soaked up her blood. Thick socks covered her feet, the sort with rubber soles to grip indoors.

"It doesn't look as if she had just arrived home and star-tled an intruder."

Garrick stood, and with a nod to follow, they left the kitchen. He walked to the front door and examined the lock.

"The security guards opened it from the inside," the officer pointed out, tagging behind him. "I think they're the keys there." She pointed to a set of hooks to the left of the door. A lone bunch of keys hung there.

Garrick nodded thoughtfully and entered the spacious living room. A large, curved floor-to-ceiling window looked across the garden. The furniture looked new, and a large 80-

inch TV hung from the wall, still connected to an Apple TV. A sideboard had a large stone carving on it. Garrick could just make out Aztec looking figures in the hewn rock. His amateurish pursuits lay with fossils, not archaeology, but he guessed the object was valuable. More artworks hung on the walls, including a large painting of angular Mayan pyramids amid a dense jungle at sunset.

He and Chib explored the rooms upstairs. Two guest bedrooms looked as if they had never been slept in. The bed in the largest room was unmade, and a pile of Kirsty's clothing was heaped on a chair. A vanity table was covered in make-up, all expensive brands as far as Garrick could tell. Putting on a blue latex glove, Garrick opened several drawers, revealing jewellery and watches.

"Found her phone," Chib said from the side of the bed. It was a Samsung Galaxy in a charging cradle. The device was locked, but the home screen picture showed a pretty blonde woman in her mid-thirties, smiling at the camera with some sort of construction work behind her.

"This is looking like the world's most inept burglary," muttered Garrick. "Either the thief lost his nerve after killing her…"

"Or it was a crime of passion," Chib finished.

Garrick hoped so. Impulsive acts of deviation were usually resolved swiftly. A partner or ex-lover seldom had the convenience of alibis or elaborate plans to conceal the facts. Most of the time they regretted their actions and confessed their sins.

A room overlooking the driveway served as an office. A PC with a large, curved screen were the only things on an otherwise empty desk. Bookshelves were crammed with volumes on ancient history. Not the sort bought from the high street, but more academic tomes. A framed photo on the wall showed Kirsty in a cap and gown, smiling on graduation day. She'd achieved a First from the Oxford School of Archaeology.

Nothing had apparently been stolen, yet something was gnawing at Garrick. Something he couldn't put his finger on. By the time he went back downstairs, the light had faded as winter approached. A security light illuminated the drive as the CSI vans finally arrived. He left Chib to oversee them and went to talk to the security guard sitting in his van listening to Heart FM.

The man was in his fifties. The black security uniform took the edge of his overweight frame. He introduced himself as Mark Cross, as he poured soup from a thermos, prepared for a long shift ahead of him. It was obvious that he'd never come across a murder before. He was still shaking and spoke in low tones as he invited Garrick to sit with him as drizzle fell.

"I need a strong drink," Mark said as he sipped his soup. Then he cast a sideways glance at Garrick. "Not that I would. Driving and all."

Garrick returned a sympathetic laugh. "Me too. Today wasn't a usual day for you then?"

"Most call outs are faults to be honest." Mark gazed at the window as fine rain blotched the window on one side, and the steam from his soup fogged up the other. "I've had a few animals trigger alarms. Usually foxes. Had a deer once. It got into the client's kitchen." He paused again as he sank deeper into his memories. "You get burglaries, of course..."

The silence extended for what felt like a full minute as they watched the Scene of the Crime Officers, wearing white overalls, dart through the rain and into the house carrying cases of equipment. Garrick finally spoke.

"What's your procedure for burglaries?"

"If we see forced entry, we call you fellas. Most of the time, intruders scarper before you arrived."

"Do you intervene?"

Mark gave Garrick a side look. "It's not our business to stop them escaping. We're paid to protect the property."

"And the owners."

Mark gave a sarcastic grunt. "When we can." His hands were shaking so much that his soup slopped over the edge. He rested the cup on the dashboard.

"Did you know her?"

"Not really. I think I met her twice. Once was a service check on the equipment. I remember she was chatty. Offered me a cuppa. That sort of thing. That's the nature of this job, being invisible. If everything's going well, we don't really get to meet the clients. I should've known this one wasn't right."

Mark shivered. Garrick got the sense that the man was blaming himself for what happened. Not wanting to interrupt the soul searching, he waited for him to continue.

"An alarm was registered as an attempted break-in. I got the call and started heading over, but then dispatch called and told me not to bother."

"Why?"

"Flanagan had called in with the safe word. She'd triggered the alarm accidentally and everything was fine."

"How safe are safe words?"

"We have two. One, a genuine safe word for false alarms. And another that clients give under duress. The operator acts normally but sends out a response team. We make people choose very different words so that they don't confuse the two."

"So if the call was cancelled, what brought you out here?"

"Twenty minutes later there was another forced entry trigger. This time she didn't call to cancel it, so I was sent out. Problem was, I was on another job in Gravesend and the traffic was bad on the way here."

"Why didn't they send somebody else?"

Mark took his soup, wrapping both hands around the cup for warmth.

"What with people off sick we're stretch thin." Garrick nodded in understanding. "Anyway. Got here. Everything looked fine. Couldn't see anything out of place. I walked around to check the back, thinking it was a false alarm. That's when I saw the kitchen door was open. I couldn't see any sign of forced entry, though. But as soon as I walked in... there she was."

He closed his eyes. A tear formed in the corner of his eyes and rolled down his cheek as his lip trembled.

"That's not a sight you ever forget. Nobody deserves that."

"We can arrange a counsellor for you if we need one." Garrick hadn't meant to sound so mechanically but he couldn't find any words to comfort him. "You saw nothing else?"

Mark shook his head. "I threw up outside and called it in. There was nothing I could do, so I sat here and locked the van doors until you lot showed up." He sipped the soup, then continued. "I stepped in the blood..." he shivered at the memory. "Those footprints are mine. Sorry."

"I know this has been a long day, but I'm going to have to ask you to hang around until my DS can take an official statement. We'll need your prints too, just for elimination." Mark nodded but said nothing.

Garrick excused himself and joined Chib as she stepped from the house. The drizzle had eased, but a damp mist hung in the air and curled through the beams of light cast by spotlights the forensic team had erected on the driveway. It made Garrick think of the iconic streetlight shot from the Exorcist movie. Mark Cross's statement had given him the feeling something was seriously amiss. The only trouble was his mind was not firing on all cylinders. The old stresses of work had been replaced by concerns about his home life. The house sale, Wendy, the baby. Usual concerns that affected most people he knew but had never troubled his own life. Where most people welcomed a return to normal, normal was a foreign land for David Garrick.

6

"Oh, come on!" Fanta exclaimed as the assembled team looked at the new crime board the very next morning. "I thought you hated coincidences?"

Garrick kept his back to the team as he pinned pictures of the bloody sledgehammer, next to a copy of Kirsty Flanagan's graduation picture. He stifled a yawn and wasn't up for trading barbs with DC Liu. By rights, Chib should be the fatigued one as she'd returned to the station directly from the crime scene after taking Mark Cross's statement and assembled the background information for this morning's briefing. Garrick had gone home, looking forward to a quiet night with Wendy, but Sonia had been there. The two had been drinking wine and discussing... well he wasn't too sure, but they were as thick as thieves when he walked in. He playfully mentioned that he wasn't too keen on Wendy drinking while pregnant, but she'd thrown him a scornful look before icily assuring him she'd only had two small glasses. The rest of the evening was spent with him feeling very much a third wheel as he sat with them in the living room.

A text message from Molly Meyers that read, *So far, so good,* further complicated his mood. He was unsure what he should do about the proposed trip to America. He hadn't yet raised it with Wendy.

"Well?" Fanta's voice jarred him back to the room. He slowly turned with a sigh.

"Your non-missing person non-case isn't linked to this at all. Because there is nothing to link," he explained patiently.

Fanta held up her fingers to count on them. "One – a treasure map on the wall of a guy who's still not turned up. Two – an archaeologist murdered."

"This isn't a bloody Dan Brown novel," said DC Lord with a snicker.

Garrick returned to his seat and gestured to Chib. "Please..."

Chib smiled despite her fatigue and took his place at the wall. Garrick glanced around and noticed the suspicious expressions etched on Lord's and Wilkes' faces. Since it was revealed that Chib had originally been planted in the team by a MET investigation to spy on Garrick, they'd both openly expressed their distrust of her. Chib had the opportunity to leave the team but wanted to stay. Now she was pulling out all the stops to turn their attitudes back around. Even if this meant practically sleeping in the office to keep a case moving.

"Kirsty Elizabeth Flanagan was born in Exeter and graduated as an archaeologist from Oxford. She was thirty-five. Her husband, Michael, died in traffic accident five months ago. They'd met reading Archaeology in Oxford and soon became real life Indiana Joneses, digging around the world and unearthing various artifacts. She specialised in Mesoamerican culture. That's the Aztecs, Mayans, Olmecs, excreta," she added with a sly smile directed at Harry Lord.

"I knew that," he muttered in a tone that suggested he didn't.

"He was an expert in the Middle East. They made a real name for themselves on several digs around the world."

"I didn't know there was so much money in archaeology," said Lord, eyeing up a picture of the house.

"They'd written books on the subject. And when major finds are bought by museums and collectors, they got a percentage. Apparently, the house was a passion project they'd completed two years earlier. Since her husband's death, she stepped back from fieldwork and focused more on trading antiquities."

"Do we have a list of people she sold items to?" Garrick asked.

"Forensics has her phone and computer, so let's hope there's something on there. But that leads me to another point. As far as we can tell, nothing was stolen. They're still going through the scene. There is no sign of forced entry either."

"Mark Cross said there were two calls from the house," said Garrick. "Twenty minutes apart."

Chib checked her notes. Despite her young age, she still preferred to note everything in a moleskin pad, in her impeccably neat handwriting. "His company confirmed that. The first time, Kirsty answered and gave the all-clear code word. The second time no call came in. Both were triggered by the door sensors, so it was assumed there was a technical problem."

Garrick frowned. "Door sensors? So she had activated the system while still at home?"

"What's wrong with that?" said Fanta. "A woman home alone in a large house..." She shrugged as if it was obvious.

"What time were the calls?" Sean Wilkes asked.

Chib double checked her notes before writing the answer on the board as she spoke. "First one was at fifteen-sixteen. The next at fifteen-thirty-seven."

Garrick thoughtfully tapped his chin. "Still daylight. That strikes me as slightly paranoid behaviour from a woman used to travelling the world and working in remote digs. What if she was worried about somebody turning up?"

"Then she was right to be," Fanta pointed out. "And doesn't that suggest a deal or something went wrong somehow?"

"Has forensics come up with what happened during the twenty minutes between alarm calls? Do they have a time of death?"

Chib raised a hand to slow him down. "Time of death won't be helpful. It could be fifteen minutes either side of the second call."

Fanta restlessly shifted in her seat. "Which means she could have been killed straight after giving the all-clear."

"Or the intruder broke in the second time and did her in," Lord pointed out.

"If nothing's been stolen, then why kill her?" said Garrick. He had no theory of his own and wanted to see if the team could point out anything he was overlooking.

"Revenge for... something," Fanta suggested.

"A lover's tiff," said Wilkes. He caught Fanta frowning at him. "What? We don't know how close she really was to her husband. She may have been in a new relationship."

"So soon after his death?" Fanta shook her head. "When I go, I want people to mourn me for *decades*."

Harry Lord stopped himself from tossing out a sarcastic reply. They'd almost lost Fanta once before, so the threat of death was one they'd all experienced. The only sane way to deal with it was not to dwell on the pain but to mock the Fates.

Questions were orbiting Garrick's mind but flew just out of reach.

"Harry, dig into her work background and find out who she was dealing with," said Chib with her usual air of authority. "Fanta, we have some next of kin details that were on her passport. Follow those up."

Fanta gave a mock salute.

"And Sean, put together a timeline of her recent movements. Right now she seems a little reclusive, but I'm sure that's not the case."

Garrick raised a questioning finger, before lowering it and realising what a bad influence Fanta was on him. One of the flock of questions had landed.

"I want to know more about the security system. How it's triggered, how long she's had it. The security guard told me he'd been to the house twice before. Once to service the equipment. What was the other reason?"

Chib scanned through her notes, then shook her head.

"He never mentioned that to me."

"Where's the company based?"

"Rochester."

GARRICK TOOK a car from the pool. It was a battered Golf hatchback. While the inside of the vehicle had seen better days, the mechanics ensured the engine was perfectly tuned. He would have killed, or at least caused mild bodily harm, for a coffee but could not imbibe the stuff without feeling ill. Instead, he drove to a McDonald's drive-through and purchased an Egg McMuffin meal for his second breakfast, with a coke for the caffeine hit. His stomach bitterly complained, but the meal did its job and gave him an energy booster.

As he approached Rochester, Wendy's name flashed up on an incoming call. Since moving in together, they seldom phoned during the day, so he couldn't help feeling concerned as he answered.

"What's wrong?"

Wendy hesitated in confusion. "Why does there have to be something wrong? Is this a bad time?"

Annoyed at immediately jumping to negative assumptions, Garrick forced a chuckle. "Sorry. One of those days. Just driving right now."

"We got our date!"

"For…?"

"The baby scan. Next Tuesday at one-thirty."

"Terrific." The 'we' part of having a baby was still odd to him. Wendy was doing all the work. She would endure all the pain. As somebody who always liked to be in control and responsible, Garrick felt like a spectator and, sometimes, a fraud. He wanted to know the sex of the child, and this scan would determine it. He knew he needed to be at Wendy's side, but he couldn't guarantee where he'd be next Tuesday during an active murder investigation. However, that was a detail she didn't need to hear. "I can't wait. I'll be there."

"If it's a problem, Sonia said–"

Garrick was uneasy because she knew him so well. "Nope. It's not a problem."

"That's a relief. So, do you have a preference yet?"

Wendy had relentlessly teased him for his opinion on whether he wanted a son or daughter, but he'd diligently remained neutral. He felt it was wrong to have a firm favourite, but that didn't stop Wendy wanting a girl. He just hoped she wouldn't be disappointed if they had a son.

"A healthy, happy kid is all I really want," he assured her as he turned into an industrial estate just on the edge of the town. The Spitfire Security office was in the middle of an identical line of business units. The circular logo, with a gun blazing Spitfire was supposed to put people in mind of the Battle of Britain, conjuring a name that protected people at their direst moment. Garrick thought it looked like a cheap logistics company.

"Look, I must go. See you later. Love you." The final words tumbled out on autopilot. What once had been a difficult thing to say now felt natural. It made him smile.

Aside from the logo on the building, the office was unremarkable. A buzzer at the door and a shuttered garage to the side were the only entrances. He hadn't called ahead, but the receptionist soon buzzed him in when he mentioned the Flanagan incident. The ground floor reception was sleek and modern. Posters on the wall depicted drones and state-of-the-art satellite monitoring solutions, while muscular security guards smiled at the camera. He was greeted by the owner, a bespectacled man called Walter Hertz. After telling the receptionist to bring in two coffees, Garrick was ushered into a smart office and sat on a leather sofa. Everything about the company reflected modernism, reassurance, and hint that the service wasn't cheap.

"Such terrible business," Walter said gravely. He earnestly leaned forward in his seat, arms resting on his knees and fingers steepled together. "We've had nothing like this before."

"Surely violence is inherent in the work."

"To a degree. We've had staff and clients assaulted. But never murdered. We have developed a strong reputation for protection services." Garrick could easily see through the man's comments. He was concerned about the bad press. He wondered just how much of Walter's concern was genuine versus business interest. "Obviously, we want to do whatever we can to help your investigation."

"The officer who attended the scene–"

"Mark Cross. He's off today. I thought he needed some compassionate leave."

"That's very thoughtful of you. Especially as he mentioned you are struggling when it comes to manpower."

"Did he now? Well, we've got a smaller pool of recruits to draw from since they all buggered back to Europe. Applicants need to be security vetted and trained. It's not a quick process. Then, on top of that, existing staff fall ill. So you can imagine giving anybody time off comes at a cost."

"How long has Cross worked for you?"

"Six years. I emailed his file to one of your team already."

Garrick suspected Fanta had been her usual super-efficient self.

"And how do you consider him as an employee?"

Walter bobbed his head, as if the question had never occurred to him. "A model employee. Always on time. Diligent. Trustworthy." He shook his head as further superlatives failed to come to him. "He's even made recommendations for new clients."

"And Mrs Flanagan, was she known to you?"

"Not personally. I know she was considered a high net

worth individual. She went for the gold standard package. We have many such clients in the region," he added with a hint of pride.

"What does your gold package comprise of?"

"A personal response within thirty minutes. A remote service of security equipment every week, in addition to the annual standard physical check. Twenty-four-hour personal helpline support. That means she could call any time she felt vulnerable or concerned, regardless of whether an alarm was triggered."

"Did she ever use it?"

"No."

"And what type of security sensors were in place at her home?"

Walter reached for a printout on his desk and passed it to Garrick.

"Motion sensors cover the entire house. Alarms on all exterior doors and windows. The front gate is automated and has an entry camera. And there's a second camera on the front door too."

"They're on all the time?"

"The client can disable it at any time for privacy reasons. However, after twenty-four hours, it's flagged up on our system and we contact them as a reminder to switch it back on."

"And did she ever disengage it?"

"Only once. Yesterday morning. But she put it back on by midday, so the time of the murder, it was all on. In fact, it was triggered twice. The front gate and then the kitchen window."

"That's when she called you?"

"Yes." Walter indicated an iPad on the glass table between them. He unlocked the screen and angled it so Garrick could see the open audio player. "All conversations are recorded." He tapped the play button. A ring tone sounded, answered moments later by Kirsty Flanagan. Although Garrick hadn't heard her speak, her soft West Country was obvious.

"Yes?"

The security operator, a middle-aged woman with an Estuary accent, spoke. "This is Spitfire Security. We have an alert."

"Oh... um... this is Kirsty Flanagan..." The line crackled as if she had breathed directly into the microphone. "*Itzamna*."

After a brief pause, the operator spoke again. "Thank you. Your alarm was triggered. So do you know–?"

Kirsty quickly interjected. "Everything's alright. I just set it off accidentally when I came in from the garden. Just me being clumsy. Thanks."

She hung up before the operator could get another word in. The recording stopped.

"She seemed quite curt," said Garrick.

"Sometimes clients are in the middle of something else, or maybe with friends and don't want to discuss their security matters aloud. And some people are... y'know..." He smiled, too polite to be openly critical.

"What triggered the alarm?"

"The front door."

"And there is a camera there?"

"Yes. Every interaction is recorded on the cloud."

"And what did it show?"

"Nothing. It wasn't recorded. It was deleted on-site using the security app on her phone. No backup was made to the cloud because her internet was down."

"At the same time?"

"We called her mobile, which is protocol. Apparently, her landline had been down since the day before. Our security systems have a cellular backup, just in case."

Something Cross had said, but hadn't registered at the time, suddenly dropped across Garrick's mental track.

"Mark Cross said he'd met the deceased twice. Once was to service the equipment. What was the second time?"

Walter frowned, then slowly shook his head.

"I don't think he did. I sent Cross's file to your team. We've highlighted any interaction he'd had with Mrs Flanagan or her husband. Mark Flanagan was the one who originally ordered the system. I went through the file myself. Cross has only been called out once before."

7

Garrick left Spitfire Security with more unanswered questions than he cared to have. Had Mark Cross been mistaken in how many times he'd met Kirsty Flanagan? Or had it been a slip of the tongue?

By the time he arrived back in the incident room the tranquillity had been replaced by intense bustle. Harry Lord was pinning up pictures of Mark Cross and another of a stubbled sandy-haired man in a dirty safari shirt, grinning at the camera. Michael Flanagan, Kirsty's husband.

"Why is he up there?" Garrick asked as he hung his Barbour jacket over the back of his chair.

"After he was killed in a car accident," Harry said as he limped back to take in his handiwork. "Kirsty made a lot of noise claiming it wasn't an accident."

"Why?"

"They'd been involved in an acrimonious sale of some artefact they'd discovered in Syria. I think she thought they'd been screwed on the deal."

"Syria?"

"I know, right? Sounds sus. I'm looking into his movements since then. According to investigators, the crash was just bad luck. A drunk lorry slammed into him on the M25 one night. Kirsty raised her concerns with the police, but since nothing was found. Nothing was pursued."

Garrick was dubious about putting Michael on the board.

Lord continued. "The coroner is delivering his report on Kirsty later this afternoon, but I think the cause of death is bleeding obvious."

"And forensics?"

"Still checking everything out, but so far they have found no evidence of forced entry."

Garrick shared his news about the security system. Lord pinned up a Google Earth printout of the house and placed a red dot where the body had been found. They looked at it for inspiration. The house backed onto farmer's fields, and the driveway led onto a busy A-road. Coming and going from the property would be difficult to do unnoticed, put people passing at speed wouldn't have had the time to make out details.

"Put out a request for anybody passing the house who may have caught something on a dash cam," Garrick said, although he didn't expect any results. He called over to Fanta who hadn't moved from her desk since he'd left earlier that morning.

"Spitfire sent through some files..."

"Already going through them, boss," she answered, without taking her eyes off the screen. "Not that there is much to go on. Kirsty last left the property the day before she died. She returned home at nineteen-thirty. That was the last time front gate was buzzed open."

Garrick crossed over to her. "How did Mark Cross get in?"

"He said the gate was already open."

"But she closed it when she returned home the previous evening?"

Fanta double-checked the record. "That's right."

"And her car is still missing?"

"A black Audi Q5," Fanta said with a frown. "Chib already put a call out for it." She leaned back in her seat and looked thoughtful. "So the first alarm could have been the gate being forced open. But wouldn't the system know which alarm was triggered?"

"The bloke at Spitfire said her internet was down, so maybe that confused it? But if that was the case, why would she cancel the call?"

"Because she knew her attacker," said Harry. "Classic scenario. Either of you want a brew?"

They both nodded, but their attention was on the security log on Fanta's screen. Garrick wasn't focused on the entries themselves but was imagining what was happening between each entry on the list.

"No forced entry, but the alarm goes off. That suggests she didn't want to see this mysterious visitor."

"Forensics said the gate and lock showed no signs of forced, either. But they could be triggered by somebody shaking them."

"So she didn't want to see them but let them in anyway. That gives a twenty-minute window in which they are probably talking."

"Then he bludgeons her to death and escapes in her car." Garrick held up a finger to pause her line of thought. Fanta jumped on the question forming on his lips. "But if the attacker arrived by a vehicle, then how did he take *both* cars?"

"There was more than one killer," they said in unison. It was so unexpected they both chuckled. No matter how macabre the subject, black humour was a sanity saver.

"Let's hold that thought for a moment," said Garrick as he rolled his seat next to hers and sat down. "What if he was on foot? Shaking the gate and demanding entry?"

"Then we're back to one killer."

"Play the security phone call."

There had been no time yet to organise the case file on HOLMES, so Fanta dug through her emails and double-clicked the attachment. The message played as it had on Walter's iPad.

"There. Play that part back," Garrick said immediately after the rustling sound from Kirsty's end. Fanta did so. "She's breathing heavy. Concerned, maybe?"

Fanta's smooth brow formed a rare frown. "To me it sounds as if she's covering the phone. Like when you don't want somebody to hear what's going on."

"She has a mute button."

"But it's easier if you want to suddenly cover the mic." She demonstrated quickly moving her phone from her ear, into the folds of her shirt, pressing it against her body. "Works just as well, and is faster than searching for the mute button."

"It's going to be impossible to tell if she did that by choice or not. By the time Mark Cross arrived, our killer could've been out of the county." Something occurred to Garrick. "Her phone was charging in the bedroom, which suggests a low battery and that she had time after the first call to go upstairs."

Fanta slowly turned a half-circle in her chair to face him. "Don't you think that's odd?"

"Which part, exactly?"

"Cross came out for the second alarm. Why was *that* triggered?"

"Because..." Garrick trailed off. Now he realised that was one of the intangible issues that had been nagging him.

"I need to check, but don't those gates automatically open from the inside? And Cross said it was already open... so why didn't it shut behind the killer?"

"It wasn't the gate alarm." Garrick suddenly recalled what he'd been told. "It was the kitchen window. The *window*. Not the *door*."

"The room she was standing in..."

"And it was closed when we were there. That suggests she set it off herself."

"Knowing it would trigger another response," breathed Fanta. "A call for help."

Garrick nodded. That's the destination he was heading with his theory, but it sounded hollow. Lord returned with a tray of drinks and some chocolate digestives he'd magicked up from somewhere. Garrick was hungry again, so took three of them as Fanta relayed their theories to Harry.

"You're missing another angle," he said as he sat down and took a noisy slurp from his builder's brown tea. "The killer was already there."

Fanta gave a curious *mmm*. "You mean hiding?"

"Okay then, another, another angle. I wasn't thinking of that. I thought that maybe she'd bought the killer home with her the evening before."

Garrick snapped his fingers. "The bed was unmade. Get forensics to double check it." Any signs of fresh sexual activity would quickly reveal themselves.

The glimmer that they were making some progress quickly evaporated as Garrick ran the scenarios through his head.

"But none of this changes the fact nothing was stolen. And it doesn't fit a crime of passion. At least, not a conventional one."

"I don't follow you," said Fanta.

"There were no signs of a fight or a struggle or an argument. For all we know, Kirsty could've opened the window and trigger the alarm, just because she needed air. And even then, she disabled the system to open the backdoor, which allowed the killer to escape. Why did she do that? Why didn't the killer just leave through the front door?"

Speculation had given them something to do, but they all knew that until forensics came back with some solid leads, it was all just an elaborate guessing game.

However, it didn't take too long for some interesting fragments of evidence to nudge things along.

THE SHRILL BEEP from the DVD recorder spinning up jolted Mark Cross from his reverie. He looked across the narrow table bolted to the floor of the interview room. Opposite him, Garrick gave a gentle nod to indicate the interview had begun.

As Garrick confirmed Cross's particulars, and the lawyer next to the security guard nodded in silent confirmation, Cross drifted off again. Only the gentle tapping of Garrick's pen on his notes pulled him back into the interview.

"Sorry?"

Garrick patiently circled his finger in the air as he

repeated, "I asked you to tell me about the call-out to Kirsty Flanagan's property."

Cross's eyes drifted lazily around the room as he recalled. "Usual start. The dispatcher called me. I was out in Gravesend and the traffic was a bugger, so it took longer to get there."

"Was this the first callout?"

Cross paused to think. "Second. There one about twenty minutes before, but that was cancelled, so I headed to Gravesend." He shucked a shoulder and didn't offer any further details.

"From approaching the property, can you walk me through exactly what happened? As clearly and as detailed as you can."

Cross shifted position, then gently drummed the fingers of his right hand on the desk. He didn't appear in a hurry to answer.

"On approach I thought it was unusual that the gate was open. I pulled up the drive and couldn't see anything amiss. It was raining ..." He drifted back into his internal memory. "Yeah. I pulled up. Parked where you saw me. I started the perimeter check, y'know, straight to the front door. Visual check on windows. That sort of thing. The garage was shut. Everything looked fine. I called the client to alert her I was on the property, but it just rang out then went to the answer phone."

He sipped water from his cardboard cup. He slowly swirled it, staring thoughtfully as the liquid sloshed around. Garrick watched him carefully. Cross had been in shock when they'd last spoke, but now he seemed a little out of sorts, as if he hadn't slept or was sedated. Cross drew in a long, deep breath before continuing.

"I went around the back, through the side gate on the right. It was unlocked. Circled around to the back door. Everything looked fine. Windows shut. There's a shed out the back which I passed. The padlock was on that. There's a rear door to the garage which I started to go towards, but that's when I noticed the kitchen door was open by a whisker." He held his thumb and forefinger a centimetre apart. "I made a beeline for it."

Garrick was bemused when Mark Cross walked his fingers across the desk. He was sure it wasn't the case, but he couldn't stop feeling the man was toying with him. After Cross sipped his water, he lapsed into silence until Garrick prompted him.

"And then what did you do?"

"I went inside. Saw the poor women on the floor and got the heck out of there. I called you from my van and sat tight until you arrived."

"And that's it? You saw no signs of anybody else on the grounds or in the house?" Cross shook his head. "Please speak up for the microphones."

"No."

"Can you give more details about what you saw in the kitchen?"

Cross turned away, looking revolted.

"There was blood everywhere. Floor, walls, countertop. Even the ceiling. The smell was terrible." He paused and stared at Garrick for several seconds. "I saw the hammer on the floor. But like I said, I got out, fast."

Garrick nodded and made a pretence of reading through the printed notes in front of him. He didn't need them. He just wanted to give Cross time to mull over his statement. Time to squirm.

"To get in and out of the house, what did you touch?"

Cross thought for a moment, then shook his head. "Nothing. I pulled the door open with the tip of my toe. Left it open when I got out. I didn't linger around to touch anything. I stepped in the blood, like I told you."

Garrick nodded and wrote on the paper. It was a nonsensical scribble, but it did the trick. Cross angled his head for a surreptitious look.

"Mrs Flanagan was known to you."

"Not really. She was a client, if that's what you mean?"

"But you've met before."

"I did a service on the alarm set up. Last year, but I couldn't tell you the month. It'll all be on record."

Garrick tapped his pen on a date printed in his notes.

"September eighteenth." Cross shrugged. "And when else?"

Cross frowned. "That was it, I think." He glanced at his solicitor. "Yep. That was it."

"Just the once?"

"Yes."

"How long have you worked for Spitfire Security?"

"Four years."

"Before that?"

"On the Ferries at Dover."

"For how long?"

"Seven years three months."

"And where else did your career take you?"

"I was a welder since leaving school. Did an apprenticeship, then got stuck in it." He turned to his solicitor and laughed. "Do I have to give him my whole CV?"

Garrick chuckled. "Sorry, Mister Cross. It just helps me tick boxes. And it seems your memory is impeccable."

"Part of the job. I need to be on the ball."

Garrick held the man's gaze. "I understand. But what I don't understand is how come your prints were on the hammer?"

Now it was Garrick's turn to smile.

8

The interview went swiftly sideways. Mark Cross claimed he had no recollection of touching the sledgehammer. Then he lapsed into a thoughtful Zen-like state, before amending his statement that he crouched down, so may have picked up the weapon, raising the haft a couple of centimetres before stopping himself and letting it clatter back to the floor. That seemed consistent with the palm prints the lab found. They were from the bottom side of his right hand and smudged backwards.

After that, his solicitor asked for a moment with his client, so the interview was paused, and the recording stopped. Garrick nipped to the toilet to splash cold water across his face. The interview room had felt like a cocoon, lulling him to sleep. Perhaps it was the faulty air conditioning, combined with Mark Cross's monosyllabic voice, but Garrick wasn't feeling particularly sharp. His senses felt dulled.

After six minutes, the solicitor signalled the interview could continue. As expected, Mark Cross now answered questions with a deflective series of *"no comment"* that just wasted everybody's time. The smudged print, and his reluctant admission that he'd touched the murder weapon, wasn't enough to hang a charge of suspected murder on him. Indeed, Detective Constable Wilkes had come back with information about the security van's tracking system that confirmed Cross was in Gravesend at the time of the alarm. It was improbable he could have made it to the house to confront Kirsty Flanagan. The coroner's report put her time of death at twenty minutes before Cross arrived. Although the science was proven, estimating precise times was still more of an arcane art form.

It was no surprise that the cause of death was severe traumata to the head. Presumably the back of the head judging from the way the body fell. There were an estimated six further strikes to the head. They were so severe that three of the floor tiles beneath the body had cracked as the corpse bounced across the floor with each blow. The tile underneath the sledgehammer's head was also cracked, indicating the killer had tossed it aside, rather than place it carefully to the floor. Kirsty died instantly. From lividity marks on her hands, wrists, and knees, she fell straight down. There were no additional injuries, and no defensive marks. The conclusion was that the attack was sudden.

This opened a plethora of scenarios. The killer was behind her, but from the open-plan geography of the kitchen, there was nowhere to hide. There was a cordless landline in the kitchen, but the angle the body rested indicated that she wasn't moving towards it, and her mobile was upstairs. If she was fleeing from her attacker, then why was she moving towards the corner? Standing behind her, the killer wasn't blocking her access out of the kitchen.

Forensics reported that there was no sign of anybody else

sleeping in the bedrooms, and no sign of sexual activity there or on the victim. That ruled out Lord's affair theory.

Garrick's gut was telling him she must have known the killer. Perhaps they'd had an altercation which led to a brutal and abrupt death. Chib had located the woman's parents in Portsmouth and was visiting them with a bereavement officer. Harry Lord was out tracing work connections. He'd made slow progress reaching out to members of their past digs. A lot of them couldn't be contacted, presumably they were out of the country or in some remote location. Those he spoke to told him that both Richard and Kirsty had been highly regarded and well loved.

With the business side of things, it turned out that buyers in the world of antiquities were very circumspect people. That had led an excited Fanta Liu to deep dive into the dark world of illicit artifact trading. While they had to explore every angle, and Garrick was a proponent of using the detective's best weapon – a hunch, he feared Fanta was teetering on the brink of a rabbit hole that would soak up their tight resources.

Mark Cross's attitude had irked Garrick. He couldn't tell if his slow, unfocused delivery was his natural manner or not. He was hardly the exemplary employee he'd been described as. What did he have to gain by being belligerent?

His memory appeared to be sharp when he wanted it to be, but vague most of the time. The one detail had had caught Garrick's attention was when Cross had described seeing blood spatter everywhere, including the ceiling. The relentless smashing of a human skull would undoubtably spray blood in all directions. Under pressure inside the body, it could squirt approximately fifteen centimetres vertically. Hardly enough to reach the ceiling. Any flecks there would have been flicked off the hammer's head as the killer raised it for the next stroke. On entering the room, Garrick's eyes had been drawn straight to the body, as he imagined Cross's having done. So what would make him look upwards and notice such a detail? Why, if he couldn't remember touching the murder weapon, did he remember that? Garrick had gone back to the forensic report to confirm blood had indeed reached the ceiling. It was an odd detail. And oddities were something he couldn't stand in a case.

If Mark Cross was innocent of any wrongdoing, then why the attitude? Why the discrepancies in his statement? Garrick knew painfully well that even the most honest of witnesses were victims of false memory syndrome. It was common for people to create fictitious statements that they truly believed were genuine. But he didn't think that was the case with this witness.

And there was the confusion with how many times he'd visited Kirsty Flanagan. His work record state once, which he'd confirmed in the interview, but he'd clearly mentioned a second time when they'd sat together outside Flanagan's house. Had he been in shock then and made a simple mistake?

With a sour taste in his mouth, Garrick had nothing solid to hang on his suspect, so was forced to release him.

"THE THIRD BIGGEST criminal activity in the world," Fanta reiterated.

"I thought that was wildlife crime?" Garrick chased a peanut around the takeout carton. He wasn't adept with chopsticks and had to suffer Fanta's disapproving side-eye. With Chib and Wilkes out of the office, they'd worked through lunch and the Deliveroo was a late afternoon mercy delivery. The Kung Pao chicken was spicy, but Garrick was too hungry to complain.

Fanta waved her chopsticks in a dismissive arc. "Maybe. I read that on the internet. That's not the point. Illegal antiquity smuggling is like a ten-billion-dollar business."

Garrick gave a low whistle. "We're in the wrong job."

Picking at his steak pie and chips, Harry Lord looked up from his desk. "I've seen pictures of her house, and I know she drives an Audi – which we still haven't found, but Flanagan hardly looks like she lives the life of a cartel boss."

DC Liu gave a low harrumph and scowled. Lord had always given Fanta a hard time when it came to listening to her wilder theories. When she was injured in an explosion, he'd eased off, but recently that amnesty seemed all-but forgotten. She pressed on without looking at him.

"Organised gangs loot sites from around the world, led by experts. Experts like our victim. They organise sales with rich buyers who don't like publicity and make lucrative profits."

"So you're thinking she was a corrupt Indiana Jones?" Harry scoffed.

Fanta gave him a hard stare. "There are antiques in her house. We know she traded them. Why are you so resistant to this idea?"

Harry pretended to look thoughtful. "I don't know... *maybe because nothing has been stolen?*"

"How do you know?"

Harry opened his mouth to reply but froze. The idea hadn't occurred to him. He gave a quick glance at Garrick in a silent plea for help. Garrick kept his attention on grappling a clump of rice with his chopsticks.

Fanta continued. "We need to know what she was selling

to her buyers. The lab hasn't been able to unlock her devices, so I'm hoping we can get a lead from her bank."

"So what's your theory?" Garrick asked, hoping to stop them from bickering.

"That she was trading some ill-gotten gains, and her buyer turned sour on her."

"And bludgeoned her to death."

Fanta nodded. "And made off with the treasure."

Garrick smiled. "Ah. Treasure. Detective, this," he wagged a finger at Fanta's screen where she'd surfed to an article on illicit antique trafficking, "wouldn't happen to do with the map we found in that house?"

"No, sir. That's just a normal bog-standard coincidence." She said with such mock-sincerity that it felt like a slap to the face.

Garrick closed the lid of his polystyrene carton and tossed it onto the table. "As much as we hate, as much as I loathe, coincidences... they happen."

"Or maybe she was attacked by pirates," Lord said, inflecting the last word with such a bad pirate accent that Garrick couldn't help but laugh. That won him a look from Fanta. "Ah, Fanta-girl. We be the pirates of old Kent."

"You're both morons!" Fanta blurted.

Garrick laughed again. There was a fine line between respect and insubordination, but he'd always encouraged his team to feel relaxed and able to fire out any ideas no matter how unusual. But his smile slowly faded, and with it, Fanta turned away, bracing herself for a reprimand. But there wasn't one coming.

"We have overlooked something. The murder weapon."

Harry Lord bit into the last of his pie as he spoke, spraying crumbs everywhere.

"I haven't. It's a six-pound lump hammer bought from a hardware shop. Nothing special about it. The head was worn, so it wasn't new."

"What's a lump hammer?" Fanta asked.

"Well, it's a..." Garrick trailed off. He wasn't sure.

"It means it's light enough to use with one hand. If you were going to use it with a chisel, for example. But you can also use it for some easy demolition work."

"And why has Flanagan got one? Assuming it was hers to begin with."

Nobody answered. Garrick glanced up at the ceiling tiles as he pondered the crime scene. He could almost see the bloodstains himself.

"And it was close at hand, too. If not in the house, presumably somewhere the killer could have easily found it."

"And if it isn't the victim's," Lord said slowly, dunking a fat chip into the remnants of a splodge of ketchup, "why would the killer bring it? I mean, a regular hammer would've been easier to carry and just as lethal. I'm guessing there were plenty of knives in the kitchen."

Garrick's synapses sparked, linking a detail to an imaginary one.

"The floor tiles in the kitchen were cracked."

"Sledgehammers tend to do that," Harry said as he took another chip.

Fanta nodded. "They break a lot of things. Like secret doors and tomb walls..." she immediately regretted speaking aloud and fuelling Garrick's earlier point. To her surprise, he nodded in agreement.

"Exactly. That's what you'd want one for. Breaking something open."

Lord and Fanta exchanged a puzzled look as Garrick stood up.

"Get your coats. I think it's raining."

IT WASN'T RAINING. It was pouring.

From under his Barbour's hood, the patter of rain was so loud David Garrick could barely hear DCs Liu or Lord as they trudged through Flanagan's garden. It was dark by the time they'd arrived at the crime scene. Forensics had already packed up and the front gates had been sealed with a padlock and police tape.

Their torch beams cut across the intense darkness and were highlighted in cones of fat raindrops that turned the manicured lawn into mud. Garrick's shoes sank into the morass. Cold water seeped over the rim and absorbed into his socks like they were sponges.

Harry Lord had slowly circled the back of the house, playing his flashlight over the exterior in the unlikely hope that he'd spot something the diligent SOCO team had missed. He was now crouched at the shed door. The building was thirty feet away from the house and couldn't be more than a few years old. Built from sturdy timbre, it was almost large enough to park a car in. As Garrick and Fanta spread out across the lawn, he fought to pick out Lord's words.

"It was padlocked when SOCO arrived." The padlock had since been removed by the investigators, so they could check inside. They'd read the report and seen the accompanying photographs of a tidy workbench covered in tools, some of which Garrick could identify from his amateur fossil work. Kirsty Flanagan evidentially used the space to examine any finds she'd made. Three different spades, a rake, two pick-axes, and an electric lawn mower sat in the corner. There was no sign the killer had been in here. Lord entered and found the light switch. Bright halogens lit the interior, forcing him to squint as his eyes adjusted. He crouched, running a hand across the floorboards that ran the length of the structure.

Outside, the strong illumination played through the open door and single window, lighting the area Fanta was examining where the lawn ran to a wildflower border. Garrick plunged on into the darkness, stepping off the grass and onto paving stones that daintily meandered to the end of the garden and the impenetrable farmer's wheat fields beyond. There had been no traces of somebody walking across the lawn and fleeing this way, so the investigation had focused on the front access to the house and drive. Garrick wasn't entirely sure what he was looking for. A hole in the ground would be too obvious, but the moment his foot pressed on a paving slab midway down the path, and he felt more than heard stone grinding against stone, he just knew he'd found *something*.

Garrick judged that he was about ten metres from the back of the garden. He lifted his foot and shone the light on the paving stone. It was circular, just like the others. About the size of an A3 sheet of paper, and scrubbed clean of moss and dirt. It showed no signs of being unusual other than a crack arcing in one quarter of the slab. He knelt for a closer look and traced his fingers along the fine line, towards the outer edge. A chunk of concrete the size of his thumb was missing. Placing his torch on the grass to illuminate the paving stone, he gripped either side of the slab. Mud squeezed under his fingernails and the chilly water quickly numbed his fingers. He pulled upwards – and the broken section of paving came away in his hand. Curious, he retrieved the light and angled it for a better view.

A sudden crash of foliage from the hedge at the back of the garden made him look up. There was a flash of light from the field. Garrick's torch followed a second later, catching the crops beyond moving as somebody fled.

Without thinking, Garrick used his crouched position to launch himself in pursuit.

9

By their very nature, impulsive actions were problematic. Garrick shouldered sidelong through the hedge delineating Kirsty Flanagan's garden from the farmer's field beyond, at top speed. Course branches snagged his clothing. He raised his hands to protect his face, but that didn't stop him from receiving a cluster of scrapes.

In a second he was through to the other side, and into a yet unharvested crop that came to his shoulders. Stalks snapped under his weight as he blindly pushed towards the feeling figure. He couldn't see anything but could hear movement as wheat crunched just feet ahead.

Slender stems slapped him in the face and across his mouth when he opened it to issue a warning. He'd only gone several metres when his toes caught on the uneven ground, and he pitched forward into the darkness. His left foot slipped in the damp and his wet right shoe flew from his foot. He twisted around to land on his shoulder. The torch flew from his grasp as he hit the dirt hard. If it wasn't wet, the few stones in the earth could've broken a bone. Instead, it was a softer, if painful landing.

And it was completely disorienting.

Garrick swayed as he rose. His damp sock sank into the mud with a squelch, causing him to teeter forward. He caught his balance and looked around. Wheat, blocked his view in every direction. Bent stems hinted at the direction he'd come from, and where his quarry had fled, but the path was subtle, not the cartoon corridor he'd hoped for. And without his torch he could barely see his own hands.

He pivoted around to track the sharp scuffling sounds. He ran towards them. As his sock sucked slowly out of the mud, he lost his balance again and stumbled several steps, arms windmilling as he painfully dropped to his knees.

"Dammit!" he yelled.

From behind came Fanta's voice. "Guv!?"

Garrick considered following the intruder, but it was futile.

"Over here!" he yelled back.

Fanta and Harry found Garrick after several shouted instructions. He retrieved his shoe but couldn't find the torch. He quickly explained what had happened as they returned to the broken paving stone.

"Did you get a glimpse of him?" Fanta asked.

"No. He legged it the moment I spotted him."

"Are you sure?" Harry asked with an uncharacteristic level of tact. The DC's expression was concealed behind the glare of his torch beam. "I mean, there are deer all around here. Foxes..."

"Bigfoot," sniggered Fanta under her breath.

"Unless they carry torches, then it was definitely a

person." Garrick glanced back at the dark field. He could almost feel the eyes of the unseen observer upon them. He was in a tricky position. Calling in the chopper would be overkill in his Super's eyes. It could be kids, a homeless person, or any number of relatively innocuous excuses. But why now? It reeked too much of coincidence, and Fanta had already wound him tightly up about that. So he had no valid reason to call in a horde of uniforms to sweep the area in the dead of night. If they were being watched, they were powerless to do anything about it.

Garrick sneezed as a chill ran through him. Then he lifted the remaining portion of the broken flagstone. Fanta dipped her torch down into the void. The hole was perfectly formed around a rusting open-topped metal container, the stone itself forming the lid. Water had seeped through the crack and pooled into the box, soaking a red cloth folded at the bottom.

Harry Lord produced a pair of blue latex gloves from his pocket and put one over his right hand. He carefully lifted the cloth out. Water tricked from the fabric as he took two corners and unfurled it. Nothing fell out, and dirty-stained images of a castle, a body of water and the words *Welcome to Loch Ness* revealed it was a tea towel.

"Something fragile must've been in there," Harry pointed out.

Fanta panned her light around the surrounding path. "Why hide it out here and not in the house?"

Harry replaced the towel and Garrick put the paving stone fragments back to shield it from the rain.

"Get SOCO out to this now," he instructed. "It's one thing Flanagan hiding it, but another that it was found. So we now have three options. Was she coerced to reveal its location, and the killer took it before they left. Or did they take it, then kill her?" He looked pensively at the house.

"The second option means the killer already knew about this cache," Fanta pointed out. "For my money, if the killer had taken the effort to bring along a sledgehammer, then they knew it was hidden *somewhere*. You mentioned a third option."

"It had already been emptied before the killer arrived."

Garrick stared into the darkness, hoping to get a glimpse of light from their observer. He was certain they were being watched, which meant they'd have to stay in place until SOCO arrived. And that could be hours away.

Harry moved closer to the house to get a phone signal to call forensics.

"Buried treasure," Fanta quipped. "Told you."

Garrick signed deeply. "Okay. You win. Dig deep. See if there is a connection."

GARRICK HAD THOUGHT about waiting in the car, but that would leave the rear of the house unguarded and with the phantom prowler still possibly around, he didn't want to risk it. Instead, he sat in the kitchen and relieved Harry and Fanta. Fanta headed home, intent on an early start the next morning, while Harry went home to catch a few winks before relieving Garrick at four in the morning so they could keep a constant vigil until forensics arrived at seven. It wasn't ideal, as it would mean they'd both be exhausted the following day, and Harry would only be awake for half his shift, weakening the team when they needed to really start making progress on the investigation.

Garrick boiled a kettle to prepare a cup of PG Tips he'd found. Drinking the deceased's tea wasn't textbook protocol, but it was preferable to falling asleep on the job. He kept the lights off, so he could clearly see into the garden. His phone was at hand, and he made sure several heavy kitchen implements were within easy reach should the skulker return. Especially if he was the killer.

Kirsty Flanagan's body had been removed, along with the weapon, but the blood spatters remained as dark shadows that gave off a metallic scent of blood. Garrick was used to the odour, but scent had a habit of stoking memories...

Images of Amy Harman flashed through his mind. The psychologist who had been assigned by the Force to help him deal with his sister's death, had been brutally slain in his own home. It was nothing more than a senseless, diabolical game by the so-called Murder Club. A bunch of degenerates who had butchered his sister and had decided a police detective would make an intriguing target. If it wasn't for him, Amy would still be alive. Deep down, Garrick knew that was nonsense. It wasn't his fault. Responsibility lay squarely at the feet of the killers. Yet dealing with victims for so long, he recognised that it was a natural human response to find ways of blaming oneself for tragedies.

What could I have done differently? was a common refrain.

The answer was inevitably *nothing,* but who wanted to hear that?

With life slowing down a little, moving in with Wendy and their baby on the way, Garrick had focused his mind on more pleasant things. But now, as midnight approached, sitting in a dark murder scene, the scent of blood that was awakening repressed memories.

Garrick had never been a spiritual man, nor did he

believe in the supernatural. But as he entered the witching hour, the house felt more oppressed as his imagination hinted at things lurking in the Stygian darkness.

He sipped at his black tea. The heat scolded his lips but kept him focused on reality. It was becoming more likely that Kirsty Flanagan was murdered over some deal she was making. The item in question had been stolen. Was that the buyer who disagreed with the price, or a middleman? He was sure that as soon as they had a fix on her business practises, the pieces would start tumbling into place.

But if it had been stolen, then why was somebody casing the house?

Alone, in the dark, Garrick questioned what he'd really seen. For months he'd suffered with a growth in his skull that exerted pressure on his brain and caused all manner of delusions, from visions to voices. At the time, they had felt real. Real enough to make him question his judgement on various cases. It was all amplified by the grief he was going through. Since his operation, the hallucinations faded away. Not completely, if he was being honest with himself...

And now he was chasing figures through dark fields. Had he really seen a light? Fanta and Harry hadn't, but they were otherwise engaged. They'd found no traces of a trespasser in the field, but that was to be expected until dawn.

What if there had been nobody there?

Garrick chased the thought away. He wondered if Wendy would still be awake, but she hadn't read his last text. He'd called her to say he wouldn't be back and, as usual, she was understanding and sympathetic. She'd spent the evening with her parents and had been looking forward to a bubble bath. As they'd exchanged a series of messages, he could tell the bath was making her drowsier as sentences shortened and typos were replaced by emojis. While he was happy that she was resting, he also wished he could hear her voice.

To pass the time, he flicked through the photos on his phone of him and Wendy. They were mostly selfies, with him gurning at the camera and her constantly laughing. She squinted when she laughed and little dimples formed on her cheeks. They were all visual prompts that made him feel so lucky to be with her. Even stuck in this bleak house, she made him feel wanted. A batch of photos from their last hike made him grin. The ever-enthusiastic Mike and Stu always had their arms around the shoulders of fellow walkers to urge them on. Sonia was unsmiling and placid in almost every picture. Then there was Larry, the big Jamaican who tripped into song every opportunity. Socialising with them ended the moment Garrick got back in his car after a hike. Looking at the images gave him a pang of longing to see them again for some muddled, unserious companionship. No wonder Wendy had bonded with Sonia. Perhaps she needed an outlet from the pressures of his work, too.

With a sigh, Garrick put the phone down and peered through the window. Even on low brightness, the screen had disrupted his night vision, so he had to wait while he regained it. The rain increased, pattering on the double glazing, and nothing seemed amiss beyond the glass.

The kitchen... why the kitchen?

The question popped into his mind as he looked down at the blood, now a congealed circular pool that gave no hint at the shape of the body. Straight lines protruded from the edges where the blood had flowed along the gaps in the floor tiles. A small amount had pooled against the foot of a kitchen cupboard, indicating the floor wasn't entirely level.

If the killer had retrieved the object outside, why kill her afterwards? Had he been caught, and they'd argued? From where her body had lain, the killer must've been in the room. Indeed, either she walked right past him or was chased from the hallway. Forensics had found no sign of any footprint there, or fingerprints on the inside front door latch when the killer left... if that had been the exit route.

Or had they left by the backdoor after killing Kirsty? Had she divulged the location of the hidden cache outside and then been murdered?

Garrick ran back through the autopsy report. There was no sign of a struggle. No bruising. Nothing.

The kitchen...

Garrick held his tea for warmth in both hands and slid from the stool. He slowly walked around the island to get a better perspective on where the body had been. What would he have done if confronted by an intruder?

Grabbed a knife. Yet Kirsty had moved further into the kitchen, past the knife block. She didn't move to the back door nor the hallway for a quick escape. Garrick's gaze strayed beyond the imagined body. She was heading to the corner of the kitchen, where the countertop ended at a wall. A bread bin and several empty wine bottles were there. There was a cupboard underneath, and a stone mask on the wall. It was a basic face shape with a tiny nose, and a pair of oval eyeholes and a slit for a mouth. It reminded him a little of a hockey mask, and his imagination immediately went to the fictional serial killer from the Friday the 13th movies. He could see two holes either side that a strap presumably tied to. He guessed it was a present from some nephew or niece, baked from clay during a lesson. It was certainly below par compared to the other sculptures dotted around the house.

The hollow eyes were commanding his attention.

Must be fatigued, he told himself.

He opened the cupboard and used the flashlight on his phone to illuminate the plates and chipped cups inside. Forensics would've looked through it them all. Out of curiosity he opened the bread bin and found half a multi-seed loaf in there, protected in its plastic wrapping. Why would she be hurrying towards this? Or was he veering down a line of inquiry that led to nothing, as was often the case?

Garrick was about to turn away, but the mask's hollow eyes held his attention once again. It sent a chill through him. He reached out and gently ran a finger down the imperfect surface. Then he impulsively took it off the wall. To his surprise, the mask had a straight backing to it, making it more of a head sculpture than the mask he had supposed. The backing clay was a different colour, hinting it was a later addition. He tilted it for a better look.

Something rolled inside.

He rolled it the opposite way, sliding the loose object inside. He twisted the eyeholes towards the floor and gently shook the artifact, but nothing came out. He inserted his fingers into the holes and felt a plastic rectangle that was larger than the aperture. Whatever it was, had been deliberately encased in the mask.

He took it over to the ceramic sink and put the plug in the drain. With a sharp jolt, he cracked the back of the mask against the bottom of the sink. The clay cracked open, along with a thumb-sized piece of the mask's front. A matchbox sized black plastic oblong clattered out. Is this what Kirsty was trying to fetch in her dying moments?

Holding the object between his fingertips, Garrick held it

up to the window, hoping the ambient light from the shed, which Harry had left on, would help. The plastic was jet black. As he turned it, he saw a small LED screen on the other side. It had a series of numbers at the top of the screen and an eight digit one in the middle.

That number was counting down...

10

The black tea had ratcheted Garrick's alertness up a notch, but the lack of sleep fogged his consciousness like a duvet ready to mug him. He'd made calls to Chib, Harry, then Fanta and Wilkes. Nobody had picked up. At best, he guessed Harry wouldn't be up for another three hours.

He figured the countdown was in days, hours, minutes, and seconds. If he was right, there was only one hour, eight minutes left. For what? He did not know. Had it been counting down already, or had liberating it from the mask triggered it? There were no other buttons on the device, and no obvious clue to its function other than a bulky timer.

He placed it on the kitchen island and stared at the smaller numbers at the top of the screen.

Kirsty Flanagan must have been trying to reach this. She, or somebody she was working with, had deliberately hidden the device in the clay mask. Someplace they thought it wouldn't be found. It had cost Kirsty her life, and the killer had overlooked it. The fact they hadn't turned the house over to look for it hinted that even the killer was unaware of it. Perhaps that's why they came back?

Garrick glanced out of the window. The rain hadn't eased. There was no sign of movement. Yet he imagined the watcher peering at him.

Focus, he told himself, and looked back at the smaller string of numbers. There was something familiar about their format, but so tired, he couldn't make the connection.

Then it dawned on him: 51.314505, 0.806169. His hiking group used them. They were GPS coordinates.

He used his phone to type them into Google Maps. It returned the result of a farmer's field outside Sittingbourne, at the junction of Bogle Road and Nouds Lane. He should wait until daybreak and go there with a team to excavate whatever it was.

But he had a literal ticking clock. What happened when it reached zero, he couldn't imagine, and he didn't have time to ponder. He had to go. That meant leaving the new evidence outside open for the mysterious watcher to wipe clean of incriminating clues... or would he be leading the killer to whatever he had been searching for?

The rapidly decreasing time spurred him into action. He texted the GPS location to his team and slipped the timer and his phone into his Barbour's pocket and started for the front door. Then he stopped. If he was going to be fumbling around in a field, he needed something to dig with. Harry had said there were tools in the shed. But that would mean exposing himself to whatever threat was out there, rather than head directly to his car at the front of the house. He sucked in a breath and strode out of the back door, pulling on his hood at the last moment.

The rain was deafening, masking any sound of somebody

approaching in the dark. His hood acted like blinkers, funnelling his vision towards the lit shed ahead. He glanced around and quickened his pace. He'd used a towel to dry his feet inside the house, but his socks and shoes were still damp and uncomfortable. By the time he opened the shed door and slipped inside, his toes were numb from the cold.

He selected a sturdy shovel from the corner and hunted around for a torch but couldn't find one. Gripping the shovel with both hands like a weapon, DCI Garrick darted back outside, half expecting to be assaulted. The shed light had spoiled his night vision once again, but this time he didn't linger for it to adjust. He used the light on his phone to navigate around the house, to the driveway at the front. He neared his Golf and slipped a hand into his pocket for the keys.

They weren't there.

Garrick shivered at the thought he'd lost them in the field. Glancing nervously around, he frantically patted his jacket. With each empty pocket, his heart sank. Then he heard the delightful clink of metal. For some reason, he'd put them in the inside pocket he didn't regularly use.

Throwing the spade onto the back seat, he climbed into the driver's seat. He couldn't repress the tremor of relief he felt when he locked the doors.

"Pull yourself together," he muttered to himself. The lack of sleep must be getting under his skin. As he started the engine, the squeal of the wipers across the window made him jump. He wasn't really in a fit state to drive, especially alone in heavy rain. He put the timer in the drinks holder and noticed he'd wasted eight minutes as it ticked just under an hour. With a tap of the screen, his phone's satnav activated, but took a painful forty seconds to accept his new route. His

destination was thirty-five minutes away. It would be tight.
With a last glance at his messages to make sure his team
hadn't called back, Garrick pulled away.

THE SCREECH of the wipers set Garrick's teeth on edge as they
battled against the rain. The Volkswagen Golf he'd taken
from the police pool wasn't ideal for the narrow B-roads. It
was small and fleet, but the heavy rain had flooded sections
of the road. Hitting the standing water at speed felt like a
physical blow to the vehicle. The waves of filthy water
completely obscured the windshield and forced Garrick to
halve his speed.

It all added to the time on his GPS.

In the cup holder, he saw the timer steadily ticking down.
His phone had lost the network's signal, but thankfully, the
GPS was still working. The never-ending puddles were
making his brakes soft, so navigating the tight bends became
increasingly perilous. Fortunately, because of the time and
weather, he passed only a couple of other cars, and as he
turned onto Bogle Road, he was the sole vehicle so urged the
Golf a little faster. The road itself was marginally wider than
his car and bordered by impassable bushes and trees on
both sides. He didn't slow down. His destination was dead
ahead.

That was not a smart idea. Here the floods had drained
away, leaving a layer of mud had coated the road and the
Golf's punished tyres had very little grip as he careered
towards a hard ninety-degree lefthand bend. Too late, he
slammed the brakes with both feet. The car slid sideways.
Luckily, Garrick had been trained in advanced driving tech-
niques during his time of the force. He steered into the skid

to keep control – although the Volkswagen still refused to make the turn, instead it continued in a straight line.

His headlights revealed a wall of trees ahead – and the metal gate he was hurtling straight for. He only had time to grip the steering wheel and thrust himself back in his seat to brace for impact before a horrendous sound shook the car. Two of the four horizontal bars of the access gate folded around the Volkswagen's grill. The other two snapped away, gouging through the bonnet, and shattering the windshield. Garrick was showered with pea-sized fragments of safety glass. The suspension mounts of both front wheels snapped, angling the wheels at a sharp forty-five degrees. They tore through the flimsy wheel arches with a vibrating crunch.

The car came to a sudden halt, and the engine stalled. The sharp *plink* of rapidly cooling metal played from under the bonnet like popcorn, along with a cloud of steam.

Garrick drew a long slow breath and shook the safety glass from his hair. He was in one piece, which is more than can be said for the Golf. He experimentally rocked his head from side to side but felt no pain. His adrenaline had kicked in, giving him the strength to unbuckle his belt, retrieve the timer and his phone. His door opened stiffly, and from the reflected dim interior light, he could just make out deep ruts the gate had carved down the side of the vehicle. He wobbled and caught his balance as his feet sank into the mud, up to his ankles.

The glass covers on the car's headlights were both cracked, but the lights themselves shone across the field. He leaned into the car and put them on full beam, further extending their range.

He took a couple of steps, instantly losing the shoe he'd liberated earlier. This time he didn't have time to retrieve it.

The countdown told him he had less than three minutes, and the GPS indicated he was about twenty metres away from his goal. Reaching in for the shovel, Garrick used it as a walking stick to help propel him through the ploughed field, towards his goal.

Stones and sharp root fragments stabbed through his sock, shooting tendrils of pain up his leg. But the cold soon took care of any discomfort. The wind whipped his hood off, and the rain lashed his hair, sending icy rivulets down his back. He couldn't afford to stop. Already it had taken him a minute to hobble to the exact GPS coordinates. If he'd been hoping for a large X, or even a scarecrow, to mark the spot, he was sorely mistaken. He cast his phone's flashlight over the area. There was no sign of anything buried. Pocketing the phone, he thrust the shovel into the mud and pressed it down with his one good shoe. The dirt made a sucking noise as he tossed the first load to the side and stabbed down again, then again. The one morsel of luck he had was that the car's headlights provided the illumination he needed.

Then the blade struck something metallic, about five centimetres beneath the surface. With hands trembling from the shock of the crash and the cold, he raked the shovel sideways, exposing a small metal box. He dropped to his knees and levered the shovel blade underneath. The box was the size of a biscuit tin and came free with ease. He took the timer from his pocket.

Forty-two seconds left.

He tossed the device to the side and ran his fingers around the box's exposed edge, locating a padlock.

"Bastard!" he muttered.

He picked up the shovel, holding it close to the blade, and struck the lock hard. After two blows, the lock remained intact, but the latch holding it came away. Using both thumbs, he pried the hinged lid open and gently placed the box on the ground so he could use his phone to reveal the contents.

Inside, a cheap mobile phone was taped to the lid. A wire ran from it to a glass jar gaffer taped into the corner of the box. It sat partially on top of a small brown envelope. Garrick froze. The similarity to a bomb was unmistakable.

The timer suddenly beeped.

By the time Garrick noticed the countdown had ended, the mobile phone's display suddenly lit up. Seconds later, the liquid in the jar bubbled.

He impulsively snatched the envelope from the box and threw himself face first into the dirt, covering the back of his head with his hands. For several moments he lay there allowing the rain to pelt him and the water to seep into his crotch and chest, the last patches of dry skin he had. When nothing happened, he rolled over with a distinct air of embarrassment and relief that none of his team had been present.

Smoke was rising from the box along with a sickly acrid smell. He rolled to his knees for a better look. The jar had cracked open, releasing acid into the box. It was so strong that the phone was already nothing more than shapeless discoloured plastic, its innards destroyed, and the metal box itself was hissing as it dissolved.

What injuries he would have sustained had he been close, Garrick didn't want to contemplate. He examined the sealed envelope in his hand. There was no writing on it, and it was taped closed. He wondered what on earth was inside that Kirsty Flanagan was willing to destroy it... and to die for.

11

D avid Garrick was feeling wretched for several reasons. He'd made it back to the broken Golf just as his phone's battery died, not that he had a signal. Now he didn't even have a torch to navigate out of the field. Wet and cold, he sat in the car and tried to turn the heating on, but the engine failed to turn over and when he smelled petrol, he stopped trying. Burning his shelter down was just within the remit of the bad fortune he was experiencing tonight. Despite the cold, fatigue had taken its toll, and he drifted asleep – only to be roughly woken up by Harry Lord who was leaning through the open car door wearing a look of grave concern.

"I thought you were dead, you tit!" his detective constable bellowed when Garrick sneezed in his face.

Lord drove Garrick home, listening intently to what had happened. He took the envelope with him, intending on passing it to the forensic team when they arrived at Flanagan's house. After what had happened with the acid bomb, they carefully placed the envelope in the boot, just in case that too was booby trapped.

Arriving home, Garrick threw his sodden clothes into heap in the bath and had a long warm shower. Wiping the condensation off the mirror, he was mortified to see a dozen tiny scratches across his face from where the safety glass had nicked him. He found an almost empty bottle of TCP anti-septic and used a folded piece of toilet paper to dab the wounds clean. It stung worse than the crash itself. A sneeze failed to wake Wendy, and he fell asleep the moment he pulled the duvet over him.

He woke up alone, bathed in a stream of daylight, and it took several long moments for him to assess the previous night's events. His neck, shoulders and lower back ached and he could see a bruise on his right shoulder from where the seatbelt had held him in place during the crash. He knew it was all soft tissue damage, or whiplash as they used to call it. Even sitting up in bed was painful.

He checked his phone for messages, only to discover that he'd been too tired to remember to charge it. That also meant his alarm hadn't gone off, and he was late for work. He put the phone on a rapid charge and quickly dressed. As the phone came to life, emails and text messages streamed across the screen. It seemed a lot had happened this morning.

Including him failing picking Wendy up for their baby scan.

Garrick felt as if he'd been punched in the gut. He'd completely forgotten about it. Wendy had taken the bus to Maidstone for a spot of shopping. From there, he was going to pick her up and drive to the hospital. And now he had no car.

He'd hastily called her back, only to find she was in the hospital waiting room. As usual, she was understanding, but did he imagine a trace of hardened dismay? Was she finally seeing the reality of being a detective's partner? That's what had put him off serious dating before, and he could see how it would bring even their solid relationship crashing to the ground. He called a taxi and headed straight to the hospital. Trying to check his messages in the back of the Prius was difficult, in part because the driver was a chatty Polish bloke who was far more cheerful than he had a right to be. And in part because Garrick's phone's battery had died again. He guessed the soaking it had received during the night may have killed it. Now he was car-less and without communication.

And he was late for the scan.

He burst into the room to find the sonographer cleaning the coupling agent gel from Wendy's exposed tummy. Wendy looked at him in surprise as he sneezed across the room.

"I assumed you weren't coming," she said.

"So sorry. My phone died. So?" he nodded at the ultra-sound screen.

"All healthy," the nurse said with a smile, packing the equipment away as Wendy sat up and put her white *Lusekofte* cardigan on.

"Can I see?"

The nurse shook her head. "I'm afraid not. I have another appointment and we held off, waiting for you."

Garrick was crestfallen. He held out his hand to help Wendy stand.

"And...?"

She smiled at him. "And what?"

"What is it?"

Wendy pursed her lips, then turned to retrieve her coat from over the back of a chair.

"It's a baby. You're the detective, you tell me."

With her back to him, Garrick couldn't tell if she was annoyed or just toying with him.

"Wend, come on..."

She put her coat on and looked at him as if deciding whether to speak. Then she turned to the nurse.

"So my next appointment?"

"Arrange it in reception. Give it about two weeks."

Garrick knew that wasn't normal. He looked between the nurse and Wendy. Finally, Wendy sighed in defeat.

"Everything's fine. We just could tell the sex from the baby's position."

Garrick felt a glut of relief. He hadn't missed the magic moment. Well, not really.

He followed Wendy as she made another appointment, then they found a small greasy spoon café around the corner and sat down for a warm drink. Garrick ordered a sausage and egg sandwich as he was famished. He smothered it in ketchup and rapidly ate it as Wendy told him about the intricacies of the ultrasound process. She didn't appear annoyed with him, but Garrick still sensed a slight regret that she hadn't taken up Sonia on offer to accompany her. Then again, he was tired and still hungry. He ordered another sandwich and told her about his night. It was difficult not to punctuate almost every sentence with a sneeze or blowing his nose. Wendy traced a finger across one of the cuts on his face.

"You should take the day off and get some rest."

"I can't. The clock is literally ticking on this case."

"You have a cold, haven't slept, and have whiplash. Normal people pull a sickie to deal with that."

"I'll take some Ibuprofen at the station."

"Oh, you're a doctor now, are you?" There was no hiding the harshness in her tone this time. He glanced questioningly at her but had a mouthful of sandwich he was working through. "You need to look after yourself. You have responsibilities now."

Garrick slowed his chewing, partly because her words had hit home, but mostly because he couldn't think of a suitable reply. Wendy was jobless, carrying their baby, and he was technically homeless and throwing himself headfirst in all manner of dangers.

Wendy dropped another brown sugar lump into her tea and stirred it.

"You're not much use to us if you're not in one piece."

Garrick sympathised with her, but the word 'us' felt as if she was positioning the baby against him. He finished the sandwich in silence. Was she trying to start an argument? That wasn't like her, then again, he knew pregnancy came with a tsunami of mood changing hormones. Or was he just so weary that he was feeling victimised?

There wasn't much small talk left to be had. He promised her he'd try to get home as early as he could. She countered that she'd arranged to see Sonia. Again, Garrick felt defensive, as if she was passive aggressively positioning him out of things. He kissed her on the forehead and took a taxi to the station on the other side of town.

There, the day didn't get any better as he was waylaid straight into his new Super's office. Garrick hadn't been here since Drury had left, and the first thing that struck him was the redecoration. The light green paint on the walls was a little too chirpy. Framed certificates and carefully cut newspaper headlines that Superintendent Malcolm Reynolds felt his minions should know about, all drew the eye down towards an overly large desk which had a laptop to one side, and the Super's phone central to the gleaming new chrome and leather seat. A plastic cup, filled with some freshly blended healthy green slush stood on a coaster. There were no stacks of paper or dog-eared files that used to populate Drury's workspace. Everything about Reynolds screamed modern, paired to the bone, and efficient. Even the man himself was cut from the same ethos.

A slender six-foot one, he wore an immaculately pressed navy-blue suit, with a crisp white shirt underneath. The top two buttons were undone in a poor attempt to claim the boss was informal. Just one of the team. Instead, it exuded a sense of clinical sterility which was further accented by the bland office.

"DCI Garrick." Reynolds gestured to the seat opposite his. A small uncomfortable plastic affair more suited to a school. No expense had been shared. Garrick took the seat. Reynolds steepled his fingers across his chest and stared at him from under his thin, plucked eyebrows. "You're in one piece. Unlike your vehicle."

"Thank you, sir." Garrick caught Reynold's slight scowl. That set the tone for the meeting: cheery optimism in the face of a dressing down.

"It will probably cost more to fix the car than replace it." Reynolds' index fingers twitched in anticipation of a response, but Garrick merely gave a small nod. "And I need not remind you we live in an era of budget cuts, and frugality."

Garrick's eyes darted around the new office, but the Super was too focused on his speech.

"We cannot afford to be reckless."

"It was an accident. Wet road. Muddy. The vehicle just skidded off. Luckily, into a field."

Reynolds waved a hand to shoo the matter away. "Whatever. We will need to look into it. Dot the I's and cross the T's sort of thing."

"In such frugal, Dickensian times, that seems like a waste of resources." Garrick smiled. It wasn't returned.

"And then this acid incident?"

"As you said, luckily I wasn't hurt."

"Opening a potential IDE in public goes against every rule we have, Detective."

Garrick struggled to keep his smile in place. The Super was clearly angling for a fight and Garrick was in the state of mind to give him one. With every new boss came the age-old game of 'finding your feet'. The king or queen of the gaff either played it to be your friend, in order to settle in and quietly lace the department with their own plans; or they brashly swept in to establish their authority in the first few weeks. Raising barriers and setting impossible expectations they knew could never be met in order to give them the opportunity to express dismay and urge their underlings to do better next time. It was all psychological games. An art form honed across time, and one Garrick didn't have the patience to engage with. Especially as Reynolds sat somewhere between the two standard camps which, in Garrick's view, made him an uncertain opponent.

"It wasn't a potential explosive device until I'd opened it. There was no reason to believe that it was booby trapped."

"You were just racing to locate a box based on a ticking countdown?" Reynolds frowned. "Which part of that scenario wasn't suspicious?"

Wrestling every urge, Garrick struck his mute button. The

silence stretched out until it became uncomfortable. Reynolds chuckled and drummed his fingers across the desk, causing his wedding ring to clack on the wood. Garrick felt a twinge of sympathy for the man's poor wife.

"Well, at least there is no injury claim!"

The throbbing ache through Garrick's shoulders and lower back begged to differ.

"Well, if that's all, sir, I'm keen to get back to my team, and–"

Reynolds ploughed through that sentence. "Nobody really enjoys oversight, Detective Garrick. Alas, it is the nature of the game these days. That and efficiency. I'm aware of your team's record, of course. Significant. Very significant." Garrick couldn't decide if that was a weak compliment or dismissive. "And also of the chaos that tends to pursue you like a bad penny."

Garrick resisted the urge to un-mix his metaphors.

With a glance at his phone, Reynolds continued. "Moving forward, an external administrator will assess all expenses."

"I thought we were saving money?" Garrick said impulsively.

"You know the old mantra. Spend money to make money. We need to identify wastages." He caught Garrick's eyes darting around the office but thought better than to comment. "And while I think about it, make sure any communication with the media, about any cases, are vetted through me first."

Garrick blinked in surprise. "Really?"

"Really. I know you enjoy promoting Molly Meyers' career, but let's face it, as far as the department is concerned, it has been a one-way street."

"Press relations are important."

"You're not her agent, Detective." Reynolds snapped and leaned back in his chair. The soft creak of new leather was the only sound in the office. "I shall level with you. I've been brought in as a new broom. An efficiency drive, and all that. You've had the luck of handling our highest profile cases–"

The narrowing of Garrick's eyes was the only reaction he gave. With one word, 'luck', Reynolds had swiped aside the team's combined police experience, acute detective work, and combined physical and metal toil. That one word gave Garrick all he needed to understand how much respect was being offered. And that was very much a one-way street. And with that revelation came the understanding that this wasn't a dressing down about ruining a pool car. It was a declaration of the new-normal. Don't make waves. Don't draw attention. None of it felt like an economy drive. It felt as if pressure was being exerted from above.

The tendrils of the notorious Murder Club had stretched from a group of serial killers, infiltrated the police, the military, and potentially seeped into the hub of Government. They were all lofty strata beyond Garrick's purview. No doubt he had ruffled feathers, but he had hoped that was now somebody else's problem.

He had trouble focusing on the rest of his Super's speech. Perhaps he was taking things too literally. Seeking meaning where there was none. But that didn't shake his uneasy feeling. Perhaps it was time for him to take a sabbatical and accept Molly Meyers offer to travel to the States to finally put his sister's murder to rest.

All he had to do was quietly put the Flanagan case to bed. Stay below the radar, and not draw any unwelcome attention.

12

"How much?" Garrick said with a sinking feeling.

"That's a moot question," DC Lord mumbled as he noisily slurped his afternoon brew. He looked away as Garrick's eyes narrowed.

Chib wasn't paying attention to their exchange. She was looking at a picture of the clay mask that now hung on the investigation board. This one had been taken with studio lighting, with the object carefully placed on a display cushion. The vacant eyeholes and slit mouth brought to mind nothing more than a basic emoji, yet the plain sculpture still conveyed accusing hatred.

"That's a difficult question," she said. From what we can tell, it's priceless. She pinned another image up – the mask Garrick had broken open in the sink.

"Not anymore," said Fanta with a chuckle. She faltered under Garrick's withering glare.

Chib continued. "The first picture is a nine-thousand-year-old Neolithic mask that Kirsty and her husband excavated in Syria. Only sixteen had ever been found and this one was the oldest yet. The previous discoveries were thought to be funeral masks. This one, unlike the others, had etchings on the inside, indicating it was of extreme religious significance. This was approximately the period religion was gaining a foothold in the area. Michael Flanagan had died when they were selling the mask. It was thought to be one-of-a-kind." She tapped the photo of the mask Garrick had broken in the sink. "This is very similar. Including the carvings on the inside."

Garrick sneezed. "Is it real?"

"That's the question. The runes inside are different, so it's not an identical copy. But they had only found one."

"So why would a second be hanging on her kitchen wall?" Garrick said suspiciously.

"And modified," Chib added, tapping the fragments of broken pottery. "These masks were made to be worn. The backing to the one you found appears to have been added to contain the GPS tracker."

Wilkes spoke from the back of the office, without looking up from his computer screen. "Damn odd place to hide something inside a priceless artefact. You'd think that would be the first thing a thief would steal."

"If they'd known there was only ever discovered? It's not uncommon for academics to make copies of artifacts to study and put on display."

Garrick knew that. Virtually none of the dinosaur skeletons displayed around the world were real. They were just careful recreations of bones stored in the vaults.

"Have you actually looked at it?" Lord said dismissively. "I mean, my niece could do better. And she's six. It's a piece of crap."

Garrick was usually vocal in his dislike of art and couldn't agree more. This time he remained silent and joined Chib at the evidence wall for a better look. He was sure that deliberately breaking a priceless artefact ran counter to Superintendent Reynolds' warning about budget responsibility.

"And if it's so valuable, why would she let anybody deface it?" Mused Chib, as she stepped back to take in the evidence pinned to the wall.

"The obvious question is whether it's a fake or not," Fanta said.

Chib nodded. "We're waiting for feedback from the British Museum. They won the auction for the first one. The specialist there," she consulted her notes, "Quentin Morgan, had dealt with the Flanagans in the past. If anybody knows, he will."

"Harry's right. It looks crap," said Wilkes. Everybody turned to look at him. He smirked and shucked a shoulder. "Well, it does. I mean, if I was a thief breaking into a house, I wouldn't have gone for that. Hiding the tracker in that was better than hiding it in the sock drawer."

Chib pulled a face in silent disagreement. Sean Wilkes' idea made more sense to Garrick.

Garrick ran a finger across the pictures of the empty metal box hidden under the paving stone. "This box is more of a mystery. What was in it? Who knew about it?"

Fanta gave a sudden sharp laugh that echoed around the room. She was intently looking at her screen and it took several moments for her to realise everybody was now looking questioningly at her. Her cheeks flushed in embarrassment, but she swiftly composed herself.

"It's all part of the treasure hunt!"

Garrick rolled his eyes and was about to interrupt, but Fanta ploughed on.

"Whatever was hidden inside that box wasn't what the killer wanted. They wanted the GPS tracker hidden in the mask. That's what led you to another box buried in the field."

"That's not a treasure hunt, Fanta," Garrick wearily pointed out.

"She's got a point," said Wilkes. His cheeks flushed red with embarrassment as everybody turned once again to him. It wasn't the done thing to support his girlfriend in the workplace. "I mean, the killer was probably after the tracker, right? What if the box you dug up was originally in the garden and later moved to the field? To protect it."

Fanta nodded in agreement and folded her arms as she angled her seat to face her boss. "This all started with a treasure map. It's just you were too blind to see it." She waited for questions, but after fifteen seconds of mute response, she slowly angled her computer monitor so the other could see a photo Fanta had taken. Lots of papers pinned to a wall. Garrick found it vaguely familiar.

"Liam Brady's house...?" He started to say, but Fanta spoke over him.

"Yes." She used the mouse to zoom in a portion of the image. It was a map with a road slashed with an orange highlighter. A black X was marked on it. "X marks the spot!"

Her smile quickly dissipated when the other's looked blankly at her. She tapped the X on the screen.

"That is Kirsty Flanagan's house!"

Garrick felt the blood throb in his ears to almost a deafening level. Fanta excitedly pressed on.

"The bloody shovel led us to Brady's place, right? Then there's all these maps, but no crime. The books on that Amazon list were all about Neolithic cultures, and a couple on Syrian history. And then, days later, a crime exactly here."

She tapped the X again. "It was staring us in the face all this time!"

"And we could've prevented a murder." The guilt hit Garrick in the gut like a sledgehammer.

Fanta was so delighted with her insight that the hard-world facts hadn't caught up. Her smile faltered and her voice cracked.

"Well, yeah. There is that... but we didn't have a crime, did we?"

Garrick couldn't blame her for framing the accusation as a question. If he hadn't told her to ignore the incident, then perhaps Kirsty Flanagan would still be alive.

Chib was already moving to her computer to access the files related to the shovel incident.

"So we have a suspect." She skimmed through the report on the screen. "Liam Brady. He was the tenant."

"But it was his blood on the shovel," Fanta pointed out. "He could also be a victim."

"Is he still missing?" Asked Garrick, his mind whirling.

Fanta nodded. "I checked in with his neighbours, and they still hadn't seen him. His landlord received the rent through a direct debit, so she's not bothered if her tenant is home or not."

"We need to put this out. Get everybody searching for him. What did he do?"

"Unemployed. He was on Universal Credit," said Fanta.

Garrick turned back to the wall. The aching throb in his neck, back and shoulders was suddenly forgotten as the strands of the case fluttered for attention, demanding to be tied together in ways that were not at all clear to the investigation team. A preventable death was bad enough, yet he couldn't help but feel a twinge of self-pity as he imagined their Super laying the blame squarely as his feet.

Coming from Liverpool, David Garrick was a natural urbanite, although living in the more rural reaches of Kent had made him turn his back on city living. As a result, he now loathed every visit he had to make into London. Although, in this instance, he was happy to have access to the British Museum, even if his beloved fossils were housed across town in the Natural History Museum.

With the sudden wave of pressure on the investigation, Garrick had come alone. His team had more pressing matters, including leading a forensic team to the house in Sittingbourne. The Southern Rail Highspeed train had taken him from Ashford International Station, into St Pancras Station in the heart of London in little over thirty-five minutes. Navigating the Piccadilly Line Tube to Russell Square was more time consuming despite it only being one stop away.

He was meeting Quentin Morgan, a specialist in Middle Eastern Neolithic culture. Quentin was in his early sixties, six-four and large with it. His tight tweed suit accentuated his ample frame. His scraggly grey hair was crowned by a bald patch and seemed to move with a life of its own as if caught in a breeze that nobody else could feel. Every time he laughed, which was often, his ample jowls jiggled hypnotically, and his perfect Etonian pronunciation echoed around his office.

While the curator was a walking stereotype, his office certainly wasn't what Garrick had expected. Rather than a plush affair that matched the grandeur of the museum, it was a plastic veneered table and a couple of threadbare stools that had been crammed at the end of an aisle in a long, windowless, storage room somewhere in the heart of the museum. The walls were lined with cabinets. Some were open, offering tantalising glimpses of deceptively deep spaces, where arcane looking artefacts lay. Quentin had explained that most of the museum's collection was archived in such storage areas. There still plenty of content waiting to be catalogued. He speculated that there were many great discoveries to be made, all lurking in the drawers of dark and foreboding museum collections.

Once seated, Quentin made small talk as they waited for an old kettle to boil, and he sloshed the water over a pair of Earl Grey tea bags. It wasn't a taste that appealed to Garrick, but he politely sipped as they spoke.

"How well did you know Mrs Flanagan?"

Quentin hugged his cup with both hands to ward off the air conditioning chill. "How well does one know anybody? I've worked with the Flanagans for several years. Mostly arranging functions with them. More with Michael who preferred the limelight. He's still sadly missed." He stared at the bubbles slowly swirling on the surface of tea, before finally adding, "And now Kirsty. Poor soul." After another pause for introspection he gave a chuckle. "They were certainly colourful characters, the pair of them."

"How so?"

"Michael thought of himself as something of an Indiana Jones figure, although he was far too lazy for any high jinks. And Kirsty... well. Fire and ice, the pair of them."

"Oh...?"

Silence reigned again. Garrick needed to tread with caution, making sure he didn't inadvertently influence the man's opinions. Unfortunately, Quentin seemed reluctant to say more. Whether from caution about bad-mouthing colleagues, or something else, he couldn't tell.

The soft hum from the air conditioning filled the void, before the curator found his words again.

"There was always tension between them. From racing to dig up the next marvel or scrapping over academic papers. Sometimes their marriage appeared to be founded on rivalry." He gave Garrick a mischievous look from under his unkempt bushy eyebrows. "Beware of academics with a grudge. They make the Cosa Nostra look pleasant." He suddenly seemed to remember he was talking to the police and his smile dropped as he bobbed an index finger at Garrick. "But they were good people, don't get me wrong. When Michael died, she was beside herself and stepped back from public appearances, academia, and even fieldwork. It shattered her world."

"And the masks, were they a joint discovery?"

Those hairy eyebrows twitched. "That depends to whom you speak to. Naturally, Michael took the credit. And to be clear, you say masks, there was only *one* – or at least one they revealed to us."

His knees cricked as he stood and put his cup down. He took a pair of blue latex gloves from a box on his desk and blew into them, inflating the rubber just enough to slide his pudgy fingers inside. Then he shuffled to a nearby display drawer and pulled it open on silent rollers. He reached in with both hands and extracted a wooden tray with a cloth over it. With reverent grace, he gently placed it on the desk.

"And here it is."

He slowly pulled the cloth back revealing an identical pagan mask to the one Garrick had broken.

"Only a few of these have been found before." He indicated several holes at either side of the mask. "A strap would have been tied here so the wearer could put it on, I think for a religious festival or rite. The others had no inscriptions on them. This, however…" he turned it over. Basic lines and shapes were etched into it; a primitive form of language now long forgotten. "Now isn't that something, he said breathlessly. Only a priest would have something like this. It's unprecedented."

"And how much is it worth?"

"Priceless, my dear boy. Priceless."

"That's hardly a figure I could see you writing on an insurance form."

Quentin hesitated. "Well, if we're narrowing things down to the level of torrid financial remuneration, the museum paid seven-hundred thousand for this."

Garrick couldn't stop himself. "For that?"

"This is no mere mask. It's an insight into a culture. A peek at the unknown. That it has survived for nine-thousand-years is remarkable. Items like this seldom turn up during one's career."

"And when did the museum acquire it?"

"We were in negotiations with Michael before… well, you know. It took another month to settle with Kirsty."

"And they potentially had another one stashed away."

Quentin gave a sigh and draped the cloth back over the mask. He carefully picked it up to return to the drawer.

"Nearly three-quarters of a million quid, and you keep it *there*?"

Quentin shrugged and gestured around one he closed the door. "When one is surrounded by the priceless, where else can it go?" He peeled the gloves off. "I don't think what you found is 'another'. Of course, proper analysis needs to be conducted, but I would wager a Ritz lunch it's a copy."

"What makes you say that?"

"The clumsily added backing. Kirsty wouldn't do that to an original piece. And why, if they had discovered additional masks, would they keep them cloaked in secrecy?"

"Have you had any interest from private collectors wanting to purchase the original mask?"

Quentin chuckled again, his eyebrows bobbing in genuine mirth. "Of course! Private collectors always come out of the woodwork, especially on new finds. They're an anathema, always driving up prices that cripple mere museum budgets. Even ours."

"Can you provide a list?"

After a thoughtful pause, Quentin's brow creased. "We don't bother tracking counter offers. There's little point. But I could get Maggie to look through email archives if that helps."

Garrick's eyes flicked about the room. He caught a few titles on book spines. Several were about Syria. "Knowing the deceased," he added the morbid detail to remind Quentin about the gravity of the situation, "can you think of any reason she would keep a copy of the mask?" He'd debated about telling the curator about the hidden cache he'd found but thought it best to keep that evidence secret for now.

The shift in Quentin's attitude was so sudden that it was almost cod-theatrical. He drummed the fingers of one hand on the desk as his eyes swiftly flittered about the room as if to check they were truly alone. His voice dropped to near audible levels.

"Mr Volkov was a frequent financier of their work. Particularly regarding the Syrian find. He was well placed to help them out there..." He trailed off and avoided Garrick's gaze.

"How so?"

"I think the correct term for Mr Volkov is an *oligarch*. Eye-wateringly rich. He's made several contributions to the museum over the years."

"Russian, I take it?"

Quentin nodded his head. "Thoroughly nice chap. If a little... eccentric."

"And you say he backed the dig that unearthed the mask?" Again, another silent nod. "Then wouldn't he have first dibs over any find? If he's a collector?"

The curator leaned back in his chair and laced his fingers across his chest, still avoiding Garrick's eyes. "One never gets involved in the contractual details of others."

"But it would be a safe assumption?"

"At times I know Michael and Volkov had fractious meetings. And over the mask, Volkov was one of the first bidders."

"I assume when you say oligarch then he'll have more money than Croesus. Surely, he could outbid the museum?"

"One would think so."

Garrick shifted position. The hard seat was making his bum go numb.

"Then what stopped him?"

Quentin forced a toothy smile and shrugged, his laced fingers rising and falling as his chest heaved.

Garrick pressed on. "Forgive my ignorance, but you are one-hundred per cent sure the mask you purchased is genuine?"

There was the subtlest twitch across the curator's face. A micro expression that most wouldn't have noticed, but

Garrick was more attuned to after decades of conducting interviews.

"My experts validated the find. We have carbon dating analysis to narrow down the precise age of such discoveries. I assure you, we are very thorough. This is the British Museum, not a used car lot."

Quentin smiled again, but this time it didn't quite reach his eyes.

13

The trip to London and back wiped out the rest of Garrick's day. Fanta had supervised the forensics team combing over Brady's rental house in Sittingbourne. They had accumulated a lot of DNA evidence that matched the dried blood on the shovel, which was to be expected. There was DNA from two other people who hadn't been flagged up on the database. Judging by the state of the house, forensics couldn't tell if the other people had lived there before Brady or were there at the same time.

Fanta was correct in identifying it was Kirsty Flanagan's house on the map pinned to the wall. That confirmed Liam Brady was investigating her. There were several other ordinance survey maps enlarged on the wall, but none of them had locations spelled out. Fanta wondered if it was to throw any other fellow treasure hunters off the trail.

As to the identity of the treasure they were hunting, it remained a mystery for now. For now there was only the other mask Garrick had damaged. Possibly a fake, but if it was genuine, then that opened a range of theories. However, there wasn't enough information to make an educational guess, and *speculation* was one of Garrick's bugbears.

There was also the issue of Brady's blood on the shove. Was he still alive? The shovel had been discarded in his own trash, which hinted that it had been an accident. Or had he been a victim leading to Kirsty Flanagan? Currently he was both victim and suspect, which wasn't helpful.

And how did Mark Cross fit into any of this, if at all? Garrick had shown Quentin a photograph of Cross, but it had rung no bells. The only other current line of enquiry was the Russian Billionaire. Wilkes had found several UK properties the oligarch owned, as well as a dozen business concerns.

DC Harry Lord had overseen further forensic work in Flanagan's house and had used the ample free time to look into the death of Michael Flanagan. He'd been killed in a fatal road accident that coincided with the sale of the mask. A forty-four-tonne lorry had ploughed head-on into him one evening. The Spanish truck driver had died instantly, and the coroner had closed the case citing the driver had fallen asleep behind the wheel.

It was a terrible accident.

Although that hadn't stopped a grieving Kirsty Flanagan from crying foul play. As far as Lord could see, she hadn't openly accused anybody, but she was insistent that it couldn't be an accident. Then the case was quickly closed, and Kirsty's pleas fell silent.

On the train back from London, Garrick sensed the team's frustration, which was further aggravated by the terrible phone reception. Even in the heart of London his phone kept losing the signal, so out in the wilds of Kent connection was almost Third World, plus he needed to keep it constantly charging from the power point in the train's seat. He shared their frustration. This was a case with many threads but no solid leads, a vague motivation, and an opaque number of victims. And right now, everything lay in the hands of the labs to find a connection.

THAT EVENING, Garrick found Wendy had invited Sonia around for dinner. They'd bought in a lasagne ready meal and had polished it off as they talked in front of the TV. Tired and feeling extremely unsociable, Garrick joined them. He was thankful when Wendy dashed away to put his dinner in the microwave, although he felt a ripple of guilt that his pregnant girlfriend was waiting on him. It also left him alone with Sonia who he'd always found a difficult conversationalist.

"Wendy says you're always busy."

"It's just one of those jobs. Y'know, somewhere there's always a crime happening." He smiled to show he was joking, even though the sentiment was true.

Sonia shrugged, causing the Pepsi in her glass to alarmingly swirl near the brim.

"That sounds awful There aren't enough police on the streets."

Garrick nodded. "Budget cuts..." he mumbled; mindful he didn't unwittingly drag himself into a political conversation he had no interest in. Over the years, he'd had enough navigating political tightropes in work, staying within narrow politically correct lines, and the inevitable tribal clashes of opinion. It made him feel tired and frustrated. In his view, politics had no place in a civilised society.

The clink of a plate being withdrawn from a kitchen cupboard, and the droning of the One Show hosts on TV masked the painful pause in conversation. Garrick racked his brain for small talk.

"Have you been on any hikes recently?" Since learning she was pregnant, he and Wendy hadn't attended any walks, although she had been to a few of the social drink mixers afterwards.

Sonia didn't seem to hear him. She gazed blankly at a space above the television and rocked the contents of her glass side-to-side.

"She told me about your sister," she suddenly said. Garrick was too surprised to reply. "Terrible thing."

If small talk was a bugbear of his, person details were the Bad Lands of conversation. From the start, Wendy had always been circumspect when it came to telling friends and family about him. Even when he appeared on TV, usually on the news and in one instance, a video that went viral across social media. She had always remained tight-lipped. To have his most vulnerable wound exposed to, for all intents and purposes, a stranger, felt like a physical wound.

When he didn't reply, Sonia glanced sidelong at him. "So you're going to America to do a film on it?"

Garrick wasn't sure how to respond. He'd briefly brought it up in conversation with Wendy, but the subject had quickly changed before they could discuss it in detail. He excused himself and ate alone in the kitchen. Only when Sonia left just after eleven, did Wendy join him in the bedroom. She had drunk more than he was comfortable with. 'Merry' would be the loving term, but Garrick wasn't feeling charitable. Sitting alone in the bedroom his temper had flared, but that ebbed as he fought against waves of tiredness. Now Wendy was in front of him, his anger had mostly been replaced by hurt. The smile on her face slipped as she correctly gauged the temperature of the room.

"What's wrong?"

"It seems you've told Sonia my life story."

Wendy frowned in confusion for a moment before her mind caught up. Her eyes widened in surprise.

"You mean about your sister?" She gave a half-smile. "Hardly your life story. It sort of slipped out. It's not as if it's a secret. It's been on the news. Your pal Molly Meyers has been using it to further her career, remember?" Her tone became frosty. A tinge of jealousy? Garrick couldn't tell, but he'd never noticed it before.

"She was reporting a story. That's one thing. It wasn't a personal expose–"

"Bollocks! Sonia's my friend and probably already knew. It just came out in conversation when I mentioned you might be going to the States to find out more. She asked nothing else. We started talking about what I might do for work once this is all over." She indicated her body.

Garrick was annoyed, especially as Wendy was factually correct. There was enough information out there because of the various Murder Club reports in the news, yet Wendy talking about it felt like a betrayal.

"It's not the point if she can Google it or not. I tell you things. Private things, Wend. Just between us. I don't expect them to be blurted to everybody when you're pissed!"

As his voice gradually rose, Wendy's cheeks became crimson, flooded by a mix of embarrassment and anger.

"Oh, now you're telling me I'm drinking too much?"

"What? No..."

"Don't you dare be an arsehole!"

Tears streamed down her cheeks. They seldom fought,

and this was probably the most vocal tiff they'd had. Either she was a terrific actor or trudging through a cocktail of hormonal induced emotions. Either way, Garrick was not prepared for the emotional assault. Nor was he prepared to back down.

"That's not what I meant–"

"You don't understand what it's like when you're not here. Coming home at all hours. I don't know if you're safe and well out there, or in some sort of danger. I don't ask either. I don't want to know!"

She turned her back to him and her shoulder shook as she sobbed. Garrick felt paralysed but summoned up the motor skills to get off the bed and gently put a hand on her shoulder. She quickly shucked it off.

"Don't!" She snapped. "I don't wanna talk to you now. I just want to sleep. Thanks for ruining what was a nice evening."

With his anger castrated, Garrick went downstairs and spent the first night on a sofa since his uni days. Wendy's outburst had done little to soothe the stab wound in his back, but as he eventually crawled into slumberland, he wondered just what he'd done wrong.

The next morning he woke extremely early and felt more exhausted than ever. He considered making Wendy breakfast in bed by way of an apology, but a stubborn streak reminded him that he wasn't the one who should be feeling contrition. So, unwashed, and still in his crumpled clothes, he headed back to the station.

14

C hecking his messages on the way into the station, Garrick was distracted by details Sean Wilkes had gathered concerning the Russian art collector, Konstantin Volkov. He had several properties around the world, but a quick check with Border Force indicated that he was still in the UK, which narrowed the search to several properties in London's Bloomsbury and Chelsea suburbs. However, there was a high likelihood that he was currently in his Surrey estate, so after a quick round of *hellos* in the office, and a matcha tea from the canteen, Garrick was back on the road with Chib, as they headed to the property in her electric car.

Garrick was still feeling vulnerable from his argument with Wendy. He checked his mobile expecting a text message, a 'hello', or anything vaguely conciliatory, but there was nothing. He concluded that she was waiting for an apology from him, and that pissed him off further.

Chib filled in the silence by talking about her wedding plans. Garrick half-listened and mumbled encouragingly as she talked about disapproval from her Nigerian-based side of the family. Garrick assured her he was looking forward to attending and promised there would be no shoptalk.

The journey up the M20, along the M26 and onto the M25 was surprisingly quick. For once there were no roadworks or queues of commuter traffic. Taking the exit, they left the motorway and were soon driving down leafy, hilly lanes that didn't feel as if they were mere suburbs of London.

The Nissan Leaf's GPS indicated the long, high wall they were passing was the perimeter of Volkov's estate. Half a mile further around a bend, a pair of great stone pillars, capped by a pair of black iron eagles, marked the entrance gate. Thick conifer trees rose like guards either side of the black steel gates. Chib pulled up and spoke through an intercom, announcing themselves. She held up her ID card to the security camera, and the line fell silent. For almost a minute, Garrick thought the man on the other end was refusing them entry. They'd gambled that showing up unannounced would put Konstantin Volkov on the back foot, forcing him to give more impulsive answers rather than a pre-planned script. Of course, they could claim he wasn't home, or the Russian could demand his lawyer attend any causal meeting. But to Garrick's relief, the voice suddenly came back with a terse: "Drive up to the house." The gate silently rolled aside, and Chib drove up the curving tarmac. Several trees blocked the view around the bend ahead, but once cleared a palatial manor house was revealed. A midnight blue Bentley Continental GT and a Porsche Cayenne, its blood red paint work barely discernible under a coating of road dirt that smeared the windows, were parked near the front door. A suited man was waiting for them at the front door. Garrick had been expecting a traditional slender, elderly butler. This guy was over six foot tall. His suit tightly tailored to his muscular frame. He had cropped black hair, and a youthful, chiselled face that belonged on a catwalk. As they approached, not even a blink punctuated the man's steely gaze. Garrick clocked a concealed earpiece in the man's right ear. He swept his gaze around the building's façade trying to spot any other security features, but they were too well hidden.

"Warrant cards, please." There was a distinct Eastern European accent. He held out his hand. Garrick and Chib swapped a look, but obliged and handed over their IDs. The man scrutinised each in turn as if memorising their warrant ID numbers. He angled the card's hologram, then cast multiple glances between their mugshots and faces, before handing them back, leaving them in no doubt he could spot a fact ID a mile away. "Follow me."

He led them through the open front door and into a spacious hallway. They were halfway across the room, heading for an adjoining corridor, before Garrick turned as the door closed behind them. A similar suited man had closed it and now stood on guard. He wondered what made Konstantin Volkov feel so insecure.

Their guide led them into a large library that Garrick judged to be the west-wing. Shelves stretched to the ten-foot-high ceiling, crammed with volumes. Some spines looked new and unopened, while others were torn and cracked. Several tables around the room held sculptures. A couple were housed in protective glass cases. Konstantin Volkov sat in a scuffed dark green wingback chair, before a large blazing fireplace. He didn't stand but smiled and gestured to a pair of chairs opposite.

"Detectives, please take a seat." His deep voice resonated

his Russian accent in almost a predatory manner, but his smile never wavered.

Garrick held out his hand to shake. "Mr Volkov, thank you for your time."

Volkov glanced at the offered hand, but instead of taking it, he clasped the arms of his chair.

"I don't like contact. I'm an old-fashioned germaphobe. No offense intended."

"None taken," said Garrick, sitting opposite. "I'm DCI David Garrick and this is Detective Sergeant Chibarameze Okon." Volkov nodded at Chib but said nothing. "Thank you for granting us the time to speak." Garrick mentally kicked himself for sounding so humble. It must be the effect of the wealth surrounding him. "We want to ask a few questions about your dealings with Michael and Kirsty Flanagan."

"Fine archaeologists. As you can tell, it is a passion of mine." He indicated the room. "I have always had a love for antiquities since I was a boy. Their work in Syria was a perfect example of why they were good. They followed hunches. Took chances. I suppose like a good police sleuth? Or at least the ones on TV."

The Russian's smile put Garrick on edge. It felt forced. Just as he was feeling uneasy, the smile suddenly dropped.

"I wanted so desperately to use those skills afterwards for a more personal quest. So when Michael died, so did my dream."

"You still had Kirsty," said Chib.

"They were a successful sum of their parts." He danced his index fingers around each other. "Ying and yang. Separately..." He flexed his fingers as if casting the Flanagans into the ether.

"What was the project you wanted them for?"

"I have always wanted to find the Amber Room." Garrick and Chib's blank expression brought the smile back. "A wonder of the world. Built by Frederick I in Prussia in 1701. Crafted from the finest Baltic amber, it moved around before finally settling in the Catherine Palace in St Petersburg. Ten years of delicate construction created a marvel. Then, in World War II, it was dismantled when the Nazis invaded."

"They stole it?"

"It vanished."

"Vanished? An entire room?"

"It took them thirty-six hours to dismantle. After that... it vanished without a trace."

"And you think they could find it for you?"

"If anybody could, the Flanagans could."

"Is that why you funded their Syrian dig?" asked Chib.

Volkov nodded. "Yes. Although I was fascinated by the site, anyway."

"And the masks they found must have meant a lot to you?" said Garrick.

"The mask was indeed quite an unexpected find."

"You must've been annoyed when they sold it to the museum."

Volkov cocked his head and shrugged dismissively. "It was their find. I merely facilitated them. Something I regret."

Garrick's brow furrowed. "Why?"

"Because it caused tensions between the two of them. Michael wanted to sell it to me. She to the museum. And Kirsty often got her way." Volkov let out a deep sigh and lightly knocked his balled fist against the chair arm. "I needed them together, not at each other's throats."

He stared into the flames. For a moment there was

nothing but the occasional pop of burning wood until Garrick broke the man's reverie.

"Kirsty though there was foul play regarding Michael's death."

Volkov pulled a face. "Of course. Anything that swayed the narrative to what she wanted."

"You didn't get along with her?"

"While they were a team, she was bearable. Alone, no. I sometimes wonder if it's worth swallowing my pride and asking her to join my quest."

Volkov gave the distinct impression he hadn't heard about Kirsty's death. Chib gave Garrick a look wondering if they should tell him. He gave a subtle nod and Chib took the lead.

"When did you last speak with Kirsty?" Chib asked in a neutral voice.

Volkov's jaw muscles clenched, and he looked at Chib under hooded eyes.

"Forgive me, Detective Sergeant. I'm used to the most underhand of business deals and can spot a leading question as it prances out of the mouth. What has happened?"

Garrick had to admire the man's bluntness. He wasn't pretending that a pair of detectives turning up at his door was usual.

"She was murdered," said Chib.

Volkov didn't bat an eyelid. "When?"

"A few days ago, in her home. We believe the thief was searching for something."

"What?" Volkov's tone had hardened.

Garrick stepped in. "I was hoping you could help us with that."

Volkov turned his palms up, he had nothing to hide. "She was not an easy woman, and the world of private antiquities is not filled with congenial old men trying to outbid one another. It's a business. Artefacts are investments that are not as volatile as gold. They only *increase* in value."

"Do you think somebody may have had a grudge against her?"

Volkov sniggered. "I think everybody she came across would have had a grudge against her. That is of no surprise. It's not uncommon for archaeologists to ratchet up prices between multiple buyers. That often leads to animosity. I can see why you wanted to talk, but as you know, business between us had already concluded. And as I have said, without her husband, she was of no interest."

Garrick nodded and forced a smile. "I understand." He gestured around the library. "I have the feeling you're something of a scholar." Volkov nodded. "Would you mind if I called to ask a few more questions as we continue our investigation? Having an expert on speed dial could be useful."

Now that his pride button had been pressed, Volkov sat more upright. "Certainly. I don't know what help I can be. I certainly don't wish to get involved with any character assassination. But if you require help, especially if you think her killer was after something she kept hidden, then don't hesitate to call me."

Numbers were exchanged, and the detectives said their goodbyes. Volkov didn't stand as the suit who greeted them now led them back to their car. Neither said a word until they pulled out of the gate.

"Well, he seemed a little eccentric," Chib said as they accelerated down the main road.

"I noticed when I said, 'masks' he kept it singular."

Chib nodded. "He knew what he was doing."

"Exactly," said Garrick thoughtfully. "He was casting just

enough shade on Kirsty, but still keeping his distance from her."

Chib looked surprised. "You think he was lying to us?"

"Not exactly. I just don't think we were asking the right questions. He wasn't evasive, he was guiding us down *his* path."

Garrick didn't know whether or not he was the one being paranoid, but he couldn't shake the feeling that Konstantin Volkov had been in control of the conversation at every turn.

"I didn't pick up on anything suspicious," said Chib.

Garrick couldn't explain it. It was more about what *wasn't* said. The gaping holes in the conversation and the lack of any clarifying answers. It was another of his damned hunches.

"Get Wilkes to run a full background check on him. How he made his money, business associates... everything."

"Okay." Chib couldn't keep the doubt out of her voice, but kept her eyes on the road.

Garrick pulled out his phone and selected Fanta's mobile number.

"In the meantime, I'm gonna ask Fanta to run a plate check."

Chib frowned. "What plate?"

"The Porsche was gone when we left. I want to know who else was home with our Russian friend."

15

"I can always count on you, Dave." Zoe's Australian accent made the words frizz with mischief, which was supported by her cheeky lopsided smile. Garrick was trying to focus on the task at hand, but his eyes kept darting to the forensic officer's hair. "What's up? Got something in your eye?"

"It's just your hair. It's a refreshing shade of... blue."

"Me natural colour, mate," she said dismissively.

Since he'd last seen her, Zoe had cut her hair into a bob and dyed it light blue. Against the white of her lab coat, it made her stand out in the brightly lit lab.

"A Forensic Smurf," Fanta piped up with a giggle. Her mirth withered under Zoe's scornful gaze.

"What was that?"

"Nothing," said Fanta with uncharacteristic meekness.

Garrick smirked when Fanta blushed and focused on the workbench. "So, the envelope..." He gestured to the brown envelope he'd recovered from the booby-trapped box. It lay on a metal tray.

"Yup. It intrigued me." Zoe pulled on a pair of blue nitrile rubber gloves. "We X-rayed the packet and it ain't rigged to blow your face off. But the box it was in, well there was little we could salvage from that. It was a basic trap, but it did its job. It wasn't designed to injure; it was designed to destroy evidence. As far as we can tell, the moment the tracker was activated, it set off the phone in the box. It was a basic pay as you go model, nothing fancy, but it did the job. When the countdown reached zero, the phone's timer sounded."

"The timer?"

"Yeah. That's the smart bit. So as soon the phone bleeped, it sent a current through the wire, which would normally power the headphones. In this case, the headphones had been cut off, and the cable rewired to a tiny explosive charge just big enough to shatter a jar of acid taped to the side."

"So the acid would destroy the envelope."

Zoe shook her head. "That's the mystery. Y'see, it was hydrochloric acid. Eats through metal, but not glass or plastic. And definitely not paper. What it did was gut the phone, SIM card 'n' all. And any DNA evidence on the phone, in the box, or on the glass."

"So what was the point of it?" Fanta asked with a trace of confusion.

Zoe indicated the envelope. "To destroy what's in the envelope. There's something metallic in there, and I thought it best you be here when I opened it." She took a scalpel from a metal kidney dish and poised the blade on the very edge of the envelope. "It's intrigued the hell outta me. That's a lot of trouble to go to, to protect a piece of metal. The area around that field is a cell spot dead zone. Everythin' except the field. So that location was chosen deliberately."

"It was just far enough away from the house to make it before time ran out," Garrick added.

Zoe slowly slid the blade across the end of the envelope and separated the narrow slip of paper. She traded the scalpel for a pair of flat-headed tweezers and a plastic stick. With one hand she inserted the stick to make the opening wider, then slid the tweezers inside and extracted a piece of silver metal about the size of a paperback novel.

Because of Fanta's enthusiasm, Garrick had been expecting some form of treasure, and the light glinting off the silver made his heart race. It was only Fanta's disappointed "*Huh?*" that brought him back to reality. Zoe laid the silver oblong next to the envelope, then checked the envelope was empty.

"If you want my professional opinion, that's a piece of baking foil."

Garrick had come to the same conclusion. It was a single layer of slightly crumpled aluminium foil.

"Is this some kind of joke?" he said, frustrated by the pain he'd gone through to retrieve it.

"The acid would've seeped through the envelope and dissolved it."

"Question is why?"

Zoe squinted and angled a desk lamp across the surface. "There could be something written on it, maybe?"

"Or on the other side," said Fanta, unable to keep the sarcasm from her voice.

Po-faced, Zoe shot her a look, then used the tweezers to flip the sheet over. The reverse side was blank too.

Zoe harrumphed. "Any more ideas, genius?"

Fanta rose to the occasion. "We're on a treasure hunt. Maybe they used invisible ink?"

Zoe pulled a face, but then hesitated. She crossed to a wall of tools hanging in neat rows and returned with a small UV flashlight. Turning the desk lamp off, she switched the flashlight on and ran the beam across the foil.

"Well, what d'you know..." Wide-eyed, she treated Fanta to a smile. "Looks like you really are a bloody detective."

Glowing ridges of a map appeared on the metal, vanishing the moment the UV light swept away. It was a detailed ordnance and survey map, hills and roads depicted with great artistic care. The only detail missing was actual place names.

Zoe was impressed. "This is a work of art."

"And a huge amount of effort," said Garrick thoughtfully.

Zoe stopped moving the light when a ghostly X appeared. She sniggered. "X marks the spot. I'll get the photo-lab in here, then we can check for any scraps left behind." She looked between Fanta and Garrick with a huge grin. "You always bring me the fun cases!"

Garrick stepped back and leaned on the workbench behind him as he tried to fit the new evidence into the bigger picture.

"Kirsty Flanagan was probably killed for whatever is under that X. Something valuable enough to go to all this effort. But then why not put it in a safe deposit box?"

"Maybe it's something too awkward to put in one. Or too big?" Fanta speculated.

"We already have a potential victim-slash-suspect, Liam Brady, whose blood was on a shovel, and was looking for this." He looked up at Zoe who was still examining the map. "Can you match soil samples from Kirsty's garden to the shovel?"

"If there were any traces left on the shovel, maybe. But

soil is pretty ubiquitous, and that's *if* there was any residue the blood hadn't washed off."

Garrick thoughtfully stroked his chin. "Did you find anything in the hole in the garden?"

Zoe turned the UV light off and cock her head at him. "Traces of rust on the tea towel used to cushion it matched the metal case this was in."

"So this really was originally hidden in her garden." said Fanta. "She must've known somebody was looking for it, so she moved it."

Garrick sighed loudly. He hadn't realised he'd done so until he noticed the other two giving him a quizzical look. "This doesn't sit right." He gestured to the map. "Assuming Kirsty Flanagan made this map, why? That would assume she knew where this mystery artefact is buried, anyway." He was loath to use the word *treasure*. "And probably buried it herself. But why? Why not keep the details in here?" He tapped the side of his head. "Who did she make the map for? Adding a self-destruct feature indicates she wanted to hide it from others, but not *everybody*. In that case, *who?*"

Fanta paced thoughtfully. "Maybe her husband made it? Then she wouldn't necessarily know what or where it was. And they could've been hiding it from anybody. How about a business partner? But one they didn't fully trust."

"Such as an investor who never got to keep his investment," Garrick speculated.

"I'd put the Russian high on the list."

"And what about Liam Brady? What's the connection?"

"None that I've found so far." Fanta cast the UV light back across the map. "How about this; the killer somehow knew this was hidden in Flanagan's garden, but she'd got wind he was closing in so moved it to the field. The killer gets frustrated when she refuses to say where she's hidden it, so she's murdered."

"Plausible," Fanta said doubtfully. "But still a lot of effort to hide something. The maps on Brady's wall led to Flanagan's house. Maybe he thought that was the end of the trail?"

"There was a lot of stuff on there we haven't had chance to look at."

Zoe circled a finger over the envelope. "Was this Flanagan woman savvy enough to put this together herself? I said it was a basic booby trap, but it took a bit of engineering to dream it up."

"Somebody with electronic skills," said Fanta as she met Garrick's eye. "Like Mark Cross."

GARRICK AND FANTA left the lab as Zoe arranged for a detailed inspection of the map. Driving back from the Russian's estate, Chib had dropped him off at the lab when Fanta had told him to meet her there. Now he was stuck with hitching a ride with DC Liu back to the station. With Fanta's edgy driving, it wasn't a journey to be relished, so he dragged his feet as they crossed the car park.

"Shall I ask Sean to bring Cross in for questioning?" said Fanta.

"We can't just haul him back for a chat without something more substantial. Plus, if he had made the device, then he could've beaten me to it."

"Unless he didn't know where it was hidden."

"Or he was trying to protect it. Whatever *it* is."

"Well, at least we have the map."

Garrick said nothing as they reached Fanta's car. She patted her pockets to locate the key. It took him several moments to latch on to what was bothering him. They were presumably now chasing the same object as the killer and were becoming distracted from their primary task of finding the actual killer.

And where did Konstantin Volkov sit in all of this? If the mask he'd broken was genuine, were there others being kept concealed for some reason? Or was it something else? And was it in any way related to Michael Flanagan's death as his wife had originally claimed, or was he the victim of an unfortunate accident?

Garrick usually felt frustrated by the untied threads of a case, but in this case it felt as if the threads were not so much disconnected, but completely unrelated.

There was another worry. Finding the map had been time critical. What was he missing now they had it in their possession? He couldn't shake the feeling that another ticking clock had been activated.

16

The weekend swept unexpectedly over Garrick, whose mind was reeling with unanswerable questions regarding the murder case. In his mind's eye, flailing strands clashed together, attempting to fuse in meaningful ways. Inevitably, they just led to logic errors, incredible assumptions, and headaches.

Fanta had traced the Porsche Cayenne's licence plate and had discovered it was registered to a private company in Cambridge. Garrick could already feel the drag of resources as he predicted they would have to wade through a series of shell companies to track down the real owner. Creating a nest of companies was a perfectly legal practise often used by the wealthy to hide assets and carried a whiff of tax evasion about it.

The unit didn't need another resource-draining activity, especially after the brief skirmish with Superintendent Malcolm Reynolds in the corridor, at the end of a slow Friday. Garrick was warned that auditors were combing his unit's every expense. Garrick had seen nobody around, so wondered just where the trollish bean counters were lurking. Perhaps under a desk? He was also left wondering just what expenses could draw such scrutiny. It was just another irritant David Garrick didn't need right now.

Returning home should have been a welcome relief, but instead he suffered a pair of speed bumps. One was an email from his conveyer warning him of a delay in the contract exchange for his house. As usual, the details were sketchy, but it ended with an optimistic *'don't worry'*, which made him fret further. Why say it if there was nothing to worry about?

And the second hitch was that he'd spent little time with Wendy since their argument. Their weekly schedule had seen to it that their brief moments together involved one or the other sleeping, or at least half-asleep and groggy. Now they had a weekend together.

The evening passed as if nothing had happened. They ordered an Indian takeout from the restaurant around the corner and ate it on the couch as tedious Friday night BBC One programming washed over them. The Butter Chicken filled Garrick with warmth and drew a blanket of slumber slowly across his body. It wasn't even ten o'clock, and he was fighting sleep as Wendy relayed conversations with her mother and Sonia, which now formed the bulk of her days. She was ambivalent about the delay in the contract exchange, pointing out that people always seemed fickle when it came to buying property. As she had never been a homeowner, Garrick sensed that she was recycling Sonia's opinions. Finally, out of the need for a hassle-free life and wanting to extinguish any potential rows over the weekend, he extended an olive branch.

"Why don't we invite Sonia and her fella over for dinner on Sunday?"

Wendy's eyes didn't drift from the TV screen, but her head angled onto his shoulder as she nuzzled closer. Garrick draped his arm around her shoulder and her natural Wendy-scent washed over him. He suddenly felt warm, relaxed, and free from any further accusations.

"She hasn't got a fella."

Garrick gave a low *mmm*, as he could've sworn that she did. Then again, that fit into her personality type. Garrick gave himself a mental slap on the wrist for such a cruel thought.

"Besides," Wendy continued, "she's going away for a couple of weeks on Monday."

Garrick wracked his brain. That rang a bell, but it also felt like a morsel of information he'd paid no heed to. He didn't want to risk souring the mood by admitting he hadn't been listening.

"Oh, yeah..." he mumbled. From the corner of his eye, he saw Wendy glance at him, but she said nothing.

You're being paranoid, he warned himself. *Learn to relax.*

As the end credits rolled on the drama they'd been watching – and one in which Garrick couldn't recall a single character name or plot point – Wendy spoke again.

"I was thinking about names today."

"Oh, yeah?"

They'd briefly discussed names in the wee hours, but it was always more of a teasing banter as they suggested the most inappropriate ones they could think of. Garrick had been holding his latest nuclear option - *Quentin* - back for the last few days. They had agreed to wait until they knew if it was a boy or a girl.

Wendy angled herself on the sofa, putting her feet up and lolling her head onto his lap so she could see his face.

"I know we've still got to wait to know what it is, but... well..."

"We're not calling her Sonia," Garrick said deadpan.

Wendy smirked and playfully slapped his arm.

"No! That'll be her middle name. I was thinking... Emilie. If it's a girl."

The mention of his sister's name was like a concrete slab falling into the path of the conversation. Unexpected and brutal. It was just after the anniversary of her death, which he'd marked in silence and Wendy hadn't commented on. He'd rolled the grief into a dark place inside his soul and got on with his life. The black date was not quite forgotten, but astutely ignored. They were never close siblings, and it made him sick to think that he thought of her more now she was dead than he ever had when she was alive.

Molly Meyer's offer to take him Stateside had kept begging his attention, but he'd been lucky to have a case baffling enough to be able to ignore it. And now, as his guard was down, and he was beginning to relax, this happened.

Wendy sensed she'd put her foot in it and squeezed his shoulder.

"I'm sorry. I–"

"No, no, no," Garrick spluttered a little too quickly. "It's fine. I just... I... um..."

"It was a thoughtless idea. Sonia mentioned it, and it sounded respectful. You know how people name their kids after grandparents, that sort of thing."

Her face flushed almost beetroot red. Garrick normally found that adorable, but right now he was mentally reeling. That it was Sonia's idea added insult to injury. He disliked her more. But it wasn't her fault. He knew that. Curiosity was an inherent human trait. It was at the core of his own profession. Perhaps if it hadn't dropped into conversation so suddenly, he would have taken it as a respectful suggestion, as he was sure it was intended.

"I feel bad now," Wendy said.

"Don't. Honestly, Wend. I was just surprised. It's a sweet idea. But... let's just see when we know. See what fits."

Wendy smiled and leaned up to peck him on the lips.

"I'll make the tea."

She rolled off the sofa and onto her feet, quickly disappearing into the kitchen. Garrick heard the kettle click on and loathed himself for hoping that their yet-to-be-born child was a boy.

THE WEEKEND PASSED IN A MALAISE. It would have been nice in any other circumstance, if it wasn't for the troubled dreams that Garrick was having with increasing frequency. And they were now following the same pattern. A terrible repeat without rhyme or reason.

WHITE.

The solid wall of snow crumbled into flakes that dashed Garrick with such force they nicked his flesh, drawing crimson slashes across this face. He raised a hand to shield his eyes from the onslaught. It felt like pins stabbing his palms, but he didn't care. He was too focused on the figure ahead.

A shadow in the snow running away from him.

Garrick called out, but his throat constricted, and only a desperate gasp escaped his lips. With his other hand he reached out, willing the figure not to flee.

Then a freak gust ripped through the blizzard revealing the vague angular forms of a ranch building. The single steel door in the side was partially open. A soft amber light within beckoning him.

Then, suddenly, he had caught up with the figure and snatched its hand. With a tug, he spun them around, revealing the startled face of his sister. Her alabaster skin almost blending her into the storm. Her eyes wide with fear.

But his attention was drawn to the hand he'd grabbed. It was wet and slick. She was missing her index and middle finger. All that was left were ragged stumps projecting from her palm. Blood flowed freely from the wounds, coiling along his own hand like probing tentacles.

He dragged his horrified gaze back to Emilie's face. Her lips were as scarlet as an open wound.

"Find me, Davy" she whispered.

Then a violent jolt pulled Emilie off her feet. She flew backwards through the air, creating a tunnel through the snowstorm as she was yanked through the open door by some supernatural force.

The metal door slammed shut with the dull thud of a tomb.

Garrick tried to scream her name as his jolted back to the land of the living.

17

I t wasn't until Monday afternoon that a fresh trickle of information came through. The first was an email from Quentin at the British Museum notifying them that, as suspected, the clay mask Garrick had broken was indeed a cheap copy. What's more, a thumbprint in the clay backing matched Kirsty Flanagan's. Whether she'd created it for any other purpose than to hide the tracker, nobody could tell.

While that information closed off several wild goose-chases, it didn't help progress the case forward. A half-hour later, details came in about the mysterious Porsche owner. Still no name had been conjured up, but there was a shell company that the deeds of the car had passed through that also owned a luxury yacht. And that yacht was currently berthed in Ramsgate.

As Garrick prepared himself to go to the marina and investigate, Fanta excitedly ran into the office with news on the treasure hunt.

"We have a location!" she beamed as she hunched over her computer to access a file.

"The map didn't have any place names on it, unless I missed something," Garrick ventured.

"I don't need them." Fanta bit her tongue as she navigated through a sea of computer folders. "Here we go." She double clicked a file, and the UV map that had been delicately created on the layer of kitchen foil appeared. Evenly lit, the forensic photographer had captured every fine detail. Details that had been painstakingly drawn using, essentially, invisible ink. "These topographic features could be anywhere in the world."

"But I bet they're right here," said Harry Lord dryly.

Fanta shot him a look to silence him, then rapped the screen with her index finger. "But somebody went to a lot of effort to add layers of detail in this. All we needed was a way to overlay this image with the real world."

Garrick joined her at the screen. "How?"

"Good old Google Earth. And with the help of lecturer at the university campus right here."

Canterbury University's Maidstone campus had an extensive television and video facility, but was also linked to sister campuses in Canterbury itself and Folkestone, that explored virtual production, gaming, and emerging technologies.

"She'd been working on machine learning and AI solutions for deep fakes, and that sort of thing." Fanta glanced between Garrick and Lord and sighed when she registered their blank faces. "It doesn't matter. It's geeky stuff. But what it means is that she'd already been working on an algorithm that could take aerial photographs and automatically match them up with geographic locations on Google Earth."

Garrick nodded, impressed despite not really understanding what she was talking about. Fanta raised a cautionary finger.

"But it's a prototype and prone to error, so we got matches in Australia, Canada, Croatia and even Africa. But," she gave Lord a sidelong glance, "we told the software to focus on the south of England. And we got a match. Right here."

She clicked another option and the map's image perfectly overlaid to a satellite image taken from Google Earth. There were swatches of trees, hills, and green rolling fields. A narrow B-road cut through the landscape, following the curves on the map.

"Where is this?"

"Snowdown." Fanta said it with a sense of awe.

Garrick shrugged. "Snowdon? As in Wales?"

"Snow*down*. It used to be a colliery. A mine. The deepest in Kent."

Garrick nodded slowly. Fanta fired facts and figures at them with mounting excitement as she called up images of long-forgotten buildings and grim mining shafts. All Garrick could think about was the claustrophobic horror of going underground.

GARRICK WAS PRESENTED WITH A QUANDARY. On one hand, this was a lead of sorts. A nudge towards discovering what the killer was seeking. On the other hand, it wasn't a direct line to establish the killer's identity. Nor was it evidence substantial enough to do anything with. Getting a warrant to search the mine would be time consuming, especially as the justification was wafer thin. Then organising a full search of the colliery would be a costly exercise, especially considering the potential danger of the site presented. It was a cost that Garrick knew he couldn't square with his Super.

Common sense told Garrick to leave Fanta's little side project to one side and focus on other matters. However, DC Fanta Liu was adamant that they had to make a cursory inspection. She argued that the root of Kirsty Flanagan's death could be there, and the killer was undoubtably after the same prize. She'd already tracked down the person in the Council who could give them permission to explore the site. And he had done so. That sealed it. Garrick was happy to delegate the task to Fanta, but knew that either he or Chib, as senior officers, should be with her. He couldn't exactly ask Chib to risk going down a decades-closed mine, at least not so close to her wedding, so he reluctantly agreed to accompany Fanta and DC Harry Lord. Wilkes and Chib would stay and gather more details about the yacht owner.

On the drive to Snowdown, in East Kent, Fanta debriefed them with information she'd mostly cribbed off the internet. Coal had been discovered in Kent back in 1890 during exploratory bores of the original Channel Tunnel, which would ultimately be completed 104 years later. The colliery in Snowdown opened in 1908 and closed 70 years later. It was the deepest in Kent, stretching down almost three-thousand feet. In its heyday, the colliery had been huge. Employing 1876 people and running an extensive train network around the coast.

Since its closure, the shafts had been capped, and the site left for nature to reclaim. The council man, Ian Traynor, had told Fanta over the phone that they occasional had requests from urban explorers to visit the site, not that permission was ever granted. Officially, nobody had been down the mine since its closure.

Snowdown itself was an unremarkable hamlet. Perhaps

the only surprising thing was that it had its own train station. Ian Traynor met them at the colliery's rusty iron gates on Holt Street. He was a rotund man, in his late fifties with a rapidly balding head, that was fenced by shabby white hair fighting for survival above his ears. He wore an ill-fitting Day-Glo green Hi-Viz jacket over a thick raincoat, and baggy jeans that were tucked into his battered steel-toe capped boots. He waved them to a parking spot next to his Renault Cleo and greeted them all with hard hats.

"Got to wear it everywhere on site," he said without preamble. "Health and safety is above the law here." He chuckled.

Bemused, Garrick took the hat and put it on. He introduced himself and his team, then looked around the barren site with a feeling of dismay. There were six large brick hangars, presumably the warehouses used to store coal before loading them onto the trains. An admin block of crumbling orange bricks lay beyond those; what was left of the slate roofs were covered in moss and weeds. Several smaller outbuildings peppered the site. The large iconic headframes that powered the lift shafts, which Fanta had shown them on the Internet, had long been dismantled. It would take a massive team days to search just the surface buildings – and that was if they knew what they were hoping to find.

Traynor led them around the site, pointing to areas and describing the history behind the mine. He clearly loved his subject and Garrick got the increasing sense that the council worker was delighted to be asked to leave his office to be here. It began to drizzle with a fine rain that seeped into everything. Garrick pulled up his Barbour's hood, which helped keep the chill from his ears, but triggered another bout of sneezing. He was already regretting coming along.

"So nobody has been here for decades?" Garrick said.

Traynor shook his head. "Not officially. Some of the local kids come in, but they know it's dangerous. They're more at home on their Xboxes. There's been talk of redeveloping the site for years now, but," he extended both arms out to take in the surrounding fields and woodland that was turning ochre in the late autumn, "there's nothing here. There's a new build in the village, well, that's over ten years old, so maybe there'll be more houses at some point. What is it you're looking for?"

"Buried treasure," Fanta blurted out with a sense of drama.

Traynor blinked in surprise and looked between the two other officers. "You are real police, aren't you?"

"Unfortunately, yes," Garrick assured him. "We have reason to believe a piece of evidence in a murder investigation may have been placed here."

That put Traynor back into serious mode and piqued his interested.

Harry Lord sneezed as the chill got to him. "'Scuse me." He blew his nose on a tissue that had been better days. "How can you tell nobody's been here?"

"Well, we can't ever be certain, but the site is covered by security." Traynor nodded towards the entrance. Garrick recalled warning signs tied to the gates but hadn't paid attention. "They check the locks and so forth."

"Could you tell if something has been disturbed?" Fanta asked him.

Traynor laughed. "No, unless it was bleeding obvious." He fished a ring of keys from his coat pocket and jangled them. "These are kept in the office, and that's where I am usually. I haven't been out here so over a year. Longer maybe, and that was with a location scout for a film."

Fanta was intrigued. "Oh, what did they shoot here?"

"Nothing. It wasn't really what they were looking for."

Garrick walked towards the nearest large building. A rusty iron gate was fixed across the large window and the huge entrance door. A tarnished padlock, the size of his palm, was clamped around a chain. The others followed behind, still talking, as he checked each building in turn. All the locks were intact and covered in a layer of rust.

The drizzle turned to rain that pattered on the exposed patchwork of cracked concrete roads that criss-crossed the site, which hadn't yet succumbed to the thigh-high weeds. Without more details, this was a colossal waste of time. Garrick turned back to the cars, intending to call it a day, especially as the light was fading, when something caught his attention.

About fifty yards away, an overgrown thicket of weeds had been crushed flat in a perfectly rectangular patch. Exactly as if a van had driven through them. He cursed his detective's curiosity and stepped closer. As he neared, it became apparent that his assumption has been correct. The dead foliage was compacted harder along the line the wheels would've taken. It stretched a dozen yards to a structure of ten-foot-high metal panels, forming a twenty-foot square barrier. A steel doorway blocked entrance. But this one had no padlock. That had been cut off and discarded in the weeds a few feet away.

"What is this?"

Traynor took the lead and examined the door, sighing with deep disapproval. "Bloody vandals. They cut right through the latch."

He opened the door towards them, revealing the darkened space beyond. He fished a small torch from his pocket and cast the beam inside.

"This," he said with a tremor of excitement. "Is the entrance to shaft three."

18

A metal cage was positioned over the lip of a shaft that had a waist-high fence around its perimeter. The red paint was flaking, but the machinery looked robust. Traynor shone his torch down the shaft. The void swallowed the beam.

"When they demolished the headstocks," he indicated upwards to where the lift would have towered over them, "they installed these construction hoists so we could still get down should the need arise."

His beam danced off a pair of iron latices bolted to the wall. They gripped a central elevator car and stretched down into the darkness.

"Is it still functional?" said Fanta, craning forward for a better view.

Garrick kept back. Already his palms were sweating and his stomach knotting. He wasn't afraid of heights. It was the depths that concerned him.

Traynor nodded. "There's a generator, but it's not kept topped up." He crossed to a control panel on the outside of the cage. He twisted a chunky black ignition switch and thumbed a red button that was covered in a grubby plastic waterproof cover. "If anybody came in here, they'd turn back–"

He flinched in surprise as the diesel generator just outside suddenly rumbled to life with a throaty cough. A light within the elevator flickered on after several false starts.

"Excuse me," he muttered and darted outside to check the genny.

Garrick, Fanta, and Lord swapped looks. DC Liu was glowing with anticipation.

"They must've gone down!"

Garrick shook his head. "No Fanta. We don't need to–"

He was cut short when Traynor dashed back.

"The genny's a quarter filled. It shouldn't be. Nobody's been here for years, and the protocol is to drain fuel so no kids can come mucking around."

Fanta's eyes widened. "There you go! Let's go and see what they've hidden down there."

She slid the cage door opened and gestured inside. Traynor raised a cautionary hand.

"Hold on a mo. There're miles of tunnels, most of them blocked off."

"We don't have to go far. But we have to try."

"And in case of flooding, the shaft needs to be checked first."

"And how would we go about that?" asked Garrick, seeing an opportunity to stall for time.

"Well," Traynor glanced at Garrick. "The primary safety officer would go down first."

Garrick gave a sharp breath as a release of tension and smiled at Fanta. "There you go. We can't break procedure."

Fanta stood arms akimbo. "And who's the primary safety officer?" she asked.

Traynor shifted from foot-to-foot. "That would be me."

Fanta beamed. "Excellent. Let's go."

Traynor hesitated for a second before his sense of adventure caught up with him and he stepped into the cage. The metal structure vibrated under his weight, but he didn't seem fazed. Fanta followed and beckoned to Garrick.

"Come on."

"It's getting dark." Garrick knew he sounded feeble.

"We're going underground. It's not going to get any lighter."

"Somebody needs to stay up here, just in case."

"Quite right, Guv." Harry Lord cleared his throat. "I'll wait for you."

Garrick met Harry's gaze. As the closest thing he had to a friend on the force, Garrick hoped he was delivering his message loud and clear through telepathy: *you bastard!*

Sucking in a deep breath, Garrick stepped into the cage. The structure trembled. The mesh floor beneath his shoes threatened to suck him into oblivion, and he felt his knees go weak.

"We're spending no more than ten minutes down there," Garrick said, desperate to keep the tremor from his voice.

"Gotcha," Lord said, moving back towards the fresh air.

"It's 2,994 feet deep. So it'll take about seven minutes down, bit longer up," Traynor nodded as he hauled the cage door closed. It clanked shut with such force the cage shook. The sound of rattling metal echoed down the shaft. "So give us half an hour."

He double-checked the cage door was secure, then hauled a chunky lever down. Motors on the side of cage buzzed into action and the hoist lowered them into the darkness with such speed that Garrick felt butterflies in his stomach. The noise was relentless, bouncing from the narrow shaft, but other than the uneven shaft sides caught in the cage's light, there was no sign of movement.

The air was thick. Not exactly stale, but there was an earthy taste lingering in Garrick's mouth. He kept his hands behind his back, fingers clenched through the mesh holes of the cage's walls and closed his eyes.

Fanta took a few pictures on her phone, but soon ran out of photographic options. Traynor switched his torch off to conserve the battery.

"When were you last down here?" Fanta said.

"Two years ago, I think. It's been a while. As far as I can remember there were no inspections on the shaft, so no reason to keep the genny topped up."

"You said there was only a quarter tank," Garrick said with sudden alarm.

"More than enough." Traynor sounded thankful Fanta had persuaded him to come down. Garrick used the long spells of silence to muster up some hideous punishment he could inflect on his young DC.

The constant whirl of the motor and the shudder of the metal holding them over the precipice, was almost hypnotic. Time felt malleable, and Garrick couldn't tell if minutes had passed or mere seconds.

"Why would anybody come down here to hide anything?" Traynor asked.

Fanta shrugged. "Because they have a wicked sense of humour? And it's a handy place if nobody comes here." She glanced around the cage. There was enough room for three other people, but it would be a squeeze. "And it suggests whatever it is, isn't massive. Like," Fanta struggled for an example, "a sarcophagus. But not something small enough to put in your pocket."

Garrick kept his eyes closed and focused on breathing. Every few feet they descended the air became thicker, almost chewy. That had to be an illusion. But it was definitely getting warmer. He unzipped his coat and could feel perspiration beading under his shirt. He couldn't shake the notion of an elevator to Hell out of his mind.

After what seemed like an hour, the elevator suddenly slowed before coming to a jarring halt at the bottom of the shaft. Garrick opened his eyes and saw only darkness. He didn't know what he was expecting, but *nothing* hadn't been a consideration.

"Here we are," Traynor said in a cheery voice as he unlatched the door lock and slid it open. As far as Garrick could tell, they were about to step out into oblivion.

Traynor switched on his torch. The beam illuminated a grubby white brick walled tunnel. Garrick blinked in surprise, convinced they'd arrived in the corridors of some abandoned Victorian sanatorium. He followed Fanta out. His feet slipping in the mud that encrusted the floor. It wasn't deep but made an echoing sucking noise with each step. His ears throbbed with the sound of his own blood coursing through them.

The corridor was about twenty feet wide, with a two pairs of rusting metal rails stretching from the elevator into the inky distance beyond the reach of Traynor's torch. Water dripped from rusting florescent light strips running width-ways above each track. Metal pipes for pumping out water, and rubber conduits housing the long-decayed wiring system, ran along the walls in waves. It was far from the image of a mine Garrick had pictured. More like an abandoned building. Despite this, his heart pounded, and he was finding it difficult to breathe.

"This reminds me of my old school," Fanta said in a near-whisper.

Traynor wiggled his light down the shaft. "It runs for quite a way down there, but it's been blocked off after about five hundred yards or so." He cast the light over the walls and floor around them. "So if anything was stashed down here, it should be close."

Fanta indicated four narrow corridors branching from the lefthand wall.

"What're those?"

"Storage rooms for spares. Medical emergencies. Miners used to have to eat and crap, um, do their business down here. You couldn't just nip upstairs for a leak."

"May I have the torch for a moment," Garrick said, extending his hand for it as he studied the floor. Traynor pressed it into his palm and Garrick crouched, angling the beam at a sharp angle over the mud layer. "If nobody's been down here for so long, then those look too fresh to me."

He ran the beam across a set of footprints that led from the elevator to the third doorway along, before returning along a similar trajectory. There were other indentations in the mud, but water had eroded them into featureless blemishes. With nothing to disturb them, these tracks were still relatively intact.

Fanta carefully crouched and took photos on her phone. She zoomed in to get details of the sole pattern and took several with her hand alongside to indicate scale. Careful not to disturb the tracks, Garrick led the way towards the third room. No doors had ever been used so red paint highlighted the openings. He cautiously stood on the threshold and shone the light around the room.

About twenty feet square, its original use was lost in time. Now it was filled with half-rotted wooden crates that gave a pungent rotting odour. They have been broken over time and tossed in here to get them out of the way. The footprints clearly led to one corner.

Garrick slowly approached, sweeping the light on the ground in front of him, fearful the floor would suddenly give way. It was a ludicrous thought as they were a kilometre underground. With one hand he toppled the wooden crates aside, revealing a dark green tarpaulin draped over a distinctive square.

Fanta closed in and carefully tugged the sheet aside, revealing something quite out of place. A new silver flight case, three feet square and five deep, with a reinforced ridge around the edges and a bumpy metal surface across the flat sections. It was more at home at a music gig than deep underground.

"That's not ours," Traynor said.

Fanta motioned to open the first latch – but Garrick reached out and grabbed her wrists to stop her.

"Remember the last box I opened?" He didn't want to use the word 'booby trap.' There was no point in alarming Traynor. "Photograph everything. We'll have to get a team down here to make sure it's safe."

Fanta was visibly annoyed at being denied immediate answers but nodded and started taking photos and videos of the case and the room. Garrick was feeling relieved. It meant they could leave this claustrophobic pit and let others clean it out. When Fanta was done, Garrick hurried them back to the cage. The ascent was much easier and lacked the foreboding unease that had accompanied him on the way down.

Reaching the surface, Garrick welcomed the cool rain that landed through his open coat and drenched his shirt. It was now dark, but DC Lord had moved his car up to the edge of the overgrown section and bathed the makeshift building in his full beam headlights. A rapid series of calls had a recovery team set to come out the following day. It would involve a bomb squad unit to ensure the case wasn't rigged, and SOCO to soak up as many details as they could.

Mindful of a wigging from his Super, Garrick judged there was no need to post an officer overnight to protect the scene. It was already being covered by a private contractor. He walked to the gates to get the name and number of the company to alert them. The torch on his phone cast across the large white 'WARNING' sign tied to the metal bars. He read it twice as the words sank in:

Spitfire Security.

The company Mark Cross worked for.

19

———

There were many issues when running a murder investigation with such a small team and restricted budget. Manpower was the obvious one, aside from the relentless multitasking the team were expected to perform. It also meant requesting extra resources not *directly* linked to the killing was like pulling teeth.

The additional resources Garrick had assumed were in place Monday morning never materialised. This brought a furious David Garrick into Reynolds' office.

"This is completely unprofessional!" Garrick yelled at his Super.

As usual, Reynold was leaning back in his chair, fingers steepled together. His only emotional response to the raised voice was his right eyebrow inching upward.

"*I'm* being unprofessional?" he replied in a low calm tone. "Detective Chief Inspector, do I need to remind you of expected protocol?"

Garrick couldn't keep the vitriol from his voice. "I believe the package we discovered could be trapped. And I remembered *your* protocol comments about the last one I opened. I also have valid reason to suspect the contents will shed light on why Flanagan was murdered. Failure to secure the evidence–"

Reynolds cut him off with a wave of a hand. "You can't just demand that resources be deployed overnight with no oversight."

Garrick sucked in a breath to calm himself. It was a horrible answer, one driven by fiscal motivation rather than the tragic human cost of a murder. But it was also one that he had no ammunition to argue against.

Reynolds seized the moral high ground. "As it happens, *after the appropriate review*, I'm willing to authorise the recovery of the evidence. Bomb disposal will be there this afternoon."

Garrick opened his mouth to retort but thought better of it.

"And should this be a wild goose chase, then you and I will be having a more intricate discussion about procedure. Do I make myself clear, Detective Chief Inspector?"

"Abundantly."

"Your track record may have cut you some slack with my predecessor, but not me. None of my staff come in here and raise their voice. Are we clear?"

The corner of Garrick's eye twitched. He really disliked this man. He should simply agree and leave, but a tiny rebellious tick itched.

"I never had cause to shout at Superintendent Drury, *sir*. She always struck me as a competent person."

The temperature in the room plummeted as Reynolds digested the insult. Again, no real emotional response broke his façade.

"Things change, Detective Chief Inspector. And my unit is no place for emotional outbursts. Particularly with *staff* whose psyche profiles need to be monitored."

Garrick began to speak but seized the initiative to shut up. His time under psychological assessment, following his sister's death and the subsequent revenge murder of his psychologist, had been closed. He'd been given the all-clear by his doctor. Reynolds was playing this trump card to keep Garrick in-line.

"Do I make myself clear?"

"Yes, sir."

Garrick left of Reynolds' office in a hurry. Back in the incident room he found maps of the colliery and the photos Fanta had taken were now on the extended evidence wall. Lord and Wilkes were on the phone. Lord's conversation was constantly punctured by his sneezes. He had accused Garrick of spreading his cold. Fanta was on her computer, leaving Chib examining the wall with a distracted expression.

"How'd it go?" she asked.

"Captain Botox is sending a recovery team to the mine in the afternoon. Make sure Wilkes or Fanta are with them."

"Botox?"

Garrick indicated to his face. "Zero emotion up here. The man's a machine." He nodded to the evidence board. "Any insights?"

"I spoke to Walter Hertz at Spitfire Security. He's sending over everything they have on the Snowdown site. They've managed the contract there for the last four years and Mark Cross had regularly patrolled it."

"And Cross?"

"I've left a message on his mobile asking if we can talk. If we turn up at his house, his solicitor will stop us dead. And there is no reason to request another interview until we have any link, other than working for the same company. Better news on the yacht, though."

"Don't keep me in suspense."

"It's registered to an Uzbekistan businessman who may have business dealings with Volkov. Bilol Umarov. We're still looking into that. But the fact the Porsche and yacht were once owned by the same shell company, and the car was at Volkov's house, I think they're friends at the very least."

"What kind of business?"

"All kinds. Telecoms, gas, mining. He's another of those oligarchs who hit the big time when the Soviet Union collapsed."

"I'll pay him a visit." Garrick forced a smile. "I've always wanted to go on a luxury yacht. Want to come?"

Chib forced a smile that didn't reach her eyes.

"What's the matter?"

"Things are moving on the case... I just wanted to remind you, it's my wedding on Friday and Saturday."

"Two days?" Garrick blinked away his surprise. "I forgot it was two days."

"Friday is a registry office. More British formal. Saturday we're going full Nigerian. Traditional dress. Party. That sort of thing."

"I'm afraid I won't be in traditional dress, Chib."

"But you're coming?"

"Saturday for sure. With Wendy. I know the others were all planning to come. I'm not sure about Friday though..."

"Of course not. I just feel, well, can you all do without me for two days?"

Garrick understood how Chib was feeling. The wedding was obviously a huge personal landmark for her, but having the team show up was a professional victory. Since it had been revealed that she'd been transferred from the MET and planted in the team to monitor Garrick, the others had felt betrayed. It hadn't been her choice, and at the time she'd seen it as a terrific career move. That was before Garrick had proved his worth and she had grown to like the team. Since then she'd worked hard to regain their trust and, as far as Garrick could tell, the others had forgiven her past choices. Except Sean Wilkes, perhaps. Garrick was sure he harboured a grudge but was kept in check by Fanta.

He smiled reassuringly. "We're all happy for you," he assured her. "And we'll cope. It'll be a struggle, but we'll manage."

That seemed to placate Chib. She glanced at Harry Lord who was still on the phone. "Maybe I should relieve Lord in tea making duties. Fancy a cuppa?"

"A matcha if you can. Then let's go yacht viewing."

Chib took orders and disappeared to fulfil them. Garrick checked his emails, his mind wandering about the registry office on Friday. He thought most Nigerians were religious but berated himself for making assumptions. His musings were interrupted by Fanta rolling her chair over to him.

"I've got something!"

"Is it catching?" he joked. Fanta didn't even break a smile. Garrick harrumphed as his shallow good mood was brought back down to earth.

"The footprints in the mineshaft."

"Flanagan's?"

"Yes."

"No surprise there. She'd obviously dreamed up this entire treasure hunt."

"But you're thinking the wrong Flanagan. The boot size is

too big for Kirsty. It matches her husband. Michael! Forensics said the conditions in the mine could easily preserve prints for over a year. It was a warm summer. Not much ground-water seeping down. They'll know more when they get there later today. But they match the size and brand of wellies found in Flanagan's shed."

The metal chair squealed as Garrick leaned back and stared thoughtfully at the ceiling.

"Michael Flanagan was hiding the case around the same time as the sale of the mask to the museum. The question now is, did his wife know? Or had he taken the information to his grave?"

"Not only that, from the maps on the wall in Brady's house, it looks like he had an inkling something was hidden underground. He just didn't know where. I found some plans for the British Museum."

Garrick looked sharply at her. "The Museum?"

Fanta nodded, thrilled with what she'd uncovered. "Which made me wonder a bunch of things."

Garrick bobbed his head to encourage her to continue.

"What if Michael and Kirsty find more than one mask on their dig? Then they argue what to do about it."

Garrick frowned. "They'd sell the whole lot, surely?"

Fanta shook her finger. "Maybe not. Several masks may be worth a lot. But are they worth more than a single, unique, artefact?"

"They were manipulating the price?"

"Think about it. A rare mask sets the market price for collectors. Then you so happened to find another one?"

"That was a big case for one mask." Garrick wasn't convinced by her logic but tried to think it through from multiple angles.

"I don't know how many more. Maybe they argue with Volkov, who was funding the expedition. They certainly argued with each other after that. And remember, Kirsty was convinced her husband's death was no accident. It makes sense if they were involved in manipulating the market. But after Michael dies, she has all the power to reveal the rest of the find and make a huge sale to private collectors. Only, she doesn't know where Michael hid the loot."

Garrick leaned back in his seat and stared at the ceiling again. It was a working hypothesis based on scant evidence and Fanta's own flight of fancy. But experience had taught him not to discount her esoteric ideas so easily. There could well be a kernel of truth wedged in there.

"That doesn't explain Bardy's connection to the victim, or victims, or our suspects."

Fanta puffed her cheeks and sighed. "Well, I know *that*. The boys are making calls to see what fits." She gestured to Lord and Wilkes. "From his Job Seeker's record I found out that Brady worked in Dover port, and I was going to go down to ask a few questions about him."

Garrick frowned, wondering why that rang a bell. "I need you at the mine when the bomb squad arrives."

"You're not going?"

Garrick looked sidelong at her. "I think you were having far more fun than I was. Chib and I have a lead on the car that was outside Volkov's house. I think that's a dead end, but we need to eliminate it." He clicked his tongue thoughtfully. "Quentin."

"Mmm?"

"The curator at the museum. It might be worth checking for links between him and Liam Brady. And Mark Cross," he added as an afterthought. He recognised he was developing an unwarranted grudge against the security man. Coincidence was no reason to pursue a suspect, but Garrick wasn't a big believer in coincidences either.

Now the case had more disconnected strands than ever before, but rather than be a frustrating distraction, Garrick sensed some of them were going to come together very quickly. Once they'd recovered the case, they'd know what it was everybody was chasing, then the heart of the investigation would finally be revealed.

20

I t took over an hour's drive from the station to Ramsgate Royal Harbour and Marina because of flooded roads and the never-ending roadworks across the county. Garrick tried to recall when the last time any of the major roads in Kent were clear and easy to drive. He couldn't, without delving into prehistory.

None of the marinas in Kent were particularly suited to berth luxury yachts, so Garrick wondered what would drive an owner to so. At best, the Royal Harbour and Marina was perfectly suitable for sports yachts and jolly runabouts for the well-heeled, of which there were plenty in the area.

As Chib parked her car and talked to the Harbour Master, Garrick clocked the Porsche Cayenne in the car park, now gleaming in the feeble sun which broke through the grey cloud cover. It was easy to spot which yacht belonged to the oligarch.

The eighty-five-foot silver vessel took up almost a whole dock, dwarfing the other vessels around it. This wasn't a luxury yacht; it was a super-yacht. The type he'd seen in movies. Standing five stories above the water with an empty helipad poking over the stern and a flag fluttering in the breeze. Garrick didn't recognise the red, white, and blue check pattern, but he'd read the report and knew the vessel was registered in Panama. The name *Perkūnas* was emblazoned on the prow.

Access to the boarding ramp was via a circuitous route around the C-shaped wooden dock. The gentle creak of boats rocking in the water and occasionally pushing against the walkway, was a constant companion, as was the shriek of gulls soaring overhead.

"Life of the rich and shameless," Garrick mumbled under his breath.

"Or the rich and corrupt," said Chib. She saw Garrick's expression. "Come on, Guv. How much do you think a boat like that costs? He bought it for thirty-eight million dollars. And that was second hand!"

"I wonder if they throw in a free helicopter for that?"

They reached the *Perkūnas'* gangplank. The smooth metal walkway extended thirty foot up to the deck. There was nobody around. The detectives exchanged glances, then Garrick smirked and called up.

"Ahoy!"

Chib sniggered and refused to meet Garrick's gaze.

"What?"

A woman appeared at the top of the ramp. She was dressed in pleated beige trousers, deck shoes and a crisp white shirt. Her mousy brown hair was in a tight ponytail that pulled the skin back over fine cheekbones. When she didn't speak, Garrick raised his warrant card.

"Detective Chief Inspector Garrick from the Kent Constabulary. We'd like to speak with Bilol Umarov."

The woman touched her ear and spoke quietly, presumably into a concealed microphone. After a moment she nodded and beckoned them.

"Come aboard," she shouted in a thick Eastern European accent.

Garrick extended his hand. "Ladies first."

He followed Chib up the steep ramp, gripping the safety chain tightly in both hands as he did so. Reaching the deck, he noticed the four gold epaulets on the woman's short sleeve. She was the captain, despite not looking older than thirty. She tilted her head for them to follow. They walked around the pristine deck, past rows of tinted windows. For such a huge vessel, Garrick was surprised there was no crew around.

Towards the prow, the captain slid a door aside and gestured inside. Garrick entered a spacious room with graceful walls curving to match the narrowing prow. The floor-to-ceiling windows flooded the area with light. In the centre, a curved sofa was positioned to offer the optimum view of the ocean ahead, which in this case was the Royal National Lifeboat Institution station, where a bright orange Severn class lifeboat was moored on the wide concrete dock.

Glass cases, mounted on plinths bolted to the floor, were filled with sculptures that looked ancient enough to be worth as much as the yacht. Even with a casual eye, Garrick could tell they spanned the globe and thousands of years of culture. That raised the question, was Bilol Umarov a co-collector with Konstantin Volkov, or were they rivals?

Umarov stood at the window, drinking a can of Red Bull. He was small, bald, and looked trim in a black tracksuit.

"British police! How charming." There was only a slight accent. He waved a finger at them. "I am a big fan of those

Midsomer Murders. John Nettles. Excellent! Welcome aboard the Perkūnas."

"The Slavic God of Thunder," said Chib with the confidence gained from a quick Wikipedia lookup at the office.

"Very good. So what brings you to me?"

"We wanted to discuss your relationship with Konstantin Volkov."

Umarov gave a good-natured chuckle. "We are like, friendly business rivals. We're both collectors." He rapped a knuckle against one of the display cases. "He always seems to inflate the price on the next find that takes my eye. Irritating. But it's only money, isn't it?"

"And that's your only business together?"

Umarov shrugged. "His fingers are in many pies, as I'm sure you know."

Garrick made a mental note to check just what pies they were.

"Mister Volkov told us about his relationship with the Flanagans. How do you know them?" It was a deliberately leading question as he had no proof that they'd ever met. He noted that the smile never left Umarov's face.

"I knew Michael before Konstantin did." He crossed to a display case. LED lights played over a long-haired, bearded wooden figurine. "They dug this up for me."

Garrick made a guess. "Thor?"

Umarov tutted. "Detective. This is Perkūnas. The Baltic god of thunder. Like Thor. They probably came from the *same* pagan origins lost in history. Every culture seems to have one: *Indra, Prian Viseh, Perun*. Legends grow to shroud facts in the fog of mystery." He patted the case. "This is very dear to me. So when Michael asked for help in Syria, I was happy to oblige."

"I thought Mister Volkov financed that dig?"

"So he did. I supplied protection." His smile broadened when Garrick and Chib exchanged a glance. "It's Syria, after all. A dangerous place these days. But one I have long had business with, so I know how to pull strings when I need to."

Garrick balanced both hands, imitating a scale. "So how did that work between you and Volkov?"

Umarov knocked back the Red Bull, then crushed the can in his fist.

"It was of no matter. I have no interest in Neolithic masks. That's not my style. Sometimes it's good to have somebody owe you a favour."

"And how were you going to have the Flanagan repay that favour?"

The Russian tossed the crushed can from one hand to the other. "When Michael died, it felt somewhat unfair to impose on poor Kirsty for anything more."

"When did you last speak to her?"

"Shortly after Michael's funeral. I don't think since." He made a point of looking thoughtful, then shook his head. "I was waiting for her to reach out to me once she had settled back into her life."

"She was looking at a career change, I believe."

Umarov regarded him steadily, as if judging just how much he should say. Garrick's instincts told him that the Russian had been holding back from the very first moment. He may be a billionaire, but his cash came from serendipity, not savant-level business acumen. It wouldn't surprise him if Umarov was a lousy businessman.

"She had her passion projects, but yes, I heard she was resting on her laurels when it came to fieldwork and was considering focusing on being a dealer."

"In your opinion, would she have made a good dealer?"

"Superb." That at least, came from the heart.

"What was her passion project?" Chib asked.

"The Mayans. She was obsessed with Boudica," said Umarov in a tone that suggested they should have known this already. "Although it wasn't a passion Michael shared, so her research always stayed on the back-burner." He glanced at the chunky Phillipe Patek watch on his wrist. "I apologise, but I have other appointments."

Garrick nodded but didn't feel in much of a rush to leave the floating luxury palace.

"One last question. In your opinion, who would have a grudge against Kirsty?"

"Bad enough to kill her?" Umarov's gaze strayed to the *Perkūnas* statue as he considered the question. "Antiquities can be a cutthroat profession. Quentin Morgan at the British Museum had a fractious relationship with her."

"Didn't he win the bid for the mask?" Chib asked.

"Exactly. He accused her of leveraging Volkov to raise the price. Morgan thinks the museum should have everything, but he still reaches out to collectors such as me, begging for donations to keep the doors open."

"And do you help out?"

"Of course. It's difficult to say no to a man like Quinten Morgan."

"Isn't he right, though?" said Garrick. "Shouldn't everybody be able to enjoy such works of art?" He pointed at the statue that had captivated the Russian.

Umarov's eyes narrow. "If that was the case, then why does the museum only show one per cent of their entire collection?" Garrick's surprised reaction made him smile.

"Oh yes. Virtually all of it is locked away in darkened vaults. At least here, the chosen few can admire history."

"What about Konstantin Volkov?" said Chib. "He funded their dig, then never got to keep the mask."

Umarov chuckled. "A delightful irony that still pisses him off. But the whole field is tainted with greed. Take Michael's last business partner. He tried to drive a wedge between husband and wife. The public may think of antiquities as a business for retirees and terrible daytime television shows. The reality is, it's a den of backstabbing and deceit. Nobody trusts anybody."

GARRICK AND CHIB ambled back along the dock to their car.

"What a delightful man," Chib said.

"He knows more than he's letting on," Garrick said checking his phone.

"About what, exactly?"

"Michael's phantom business partner, for one. I'll get Lord to see what he can dig up on that."

"Oh great, now he's inspired you to make bad archaeology puns."

When Garrick didn't answer, Chib looked at him – only to find he was a couple of yards back, standing stock still and staring at his phone.

"What's the matter?"

"About a dozen missed calls from Fanta. They went down the mine. The case has gone."

21

G arrick could hardly believe the spate of bad luck that was suddenly hounding them. The colliery was a minor detour on the way back to the station, so they met Fanta there. The bomb squad had left, and the SOCO team was setting up tents around the entrance to the number three shaft.

"I had to go down to see it for myself," Fanta said, exasperated. "The case had gone, dragged through the mud, obliterating those footprints."

"I thought security was posted here all night."

"It was. The bloke from Spitfire was parked right there." She pointed to a Spitfire Security van parked with its tail against one of the warehouses, so that the driver had a clear view towards the shaft entrance. Even from this distance, Garrick could see the broken driver's window and the beads of glass on the floor. "He was attacked. Dragged out of the car and beaten unconscious. He woke up hog-tied against the fence. He's been taken to hospital but says he didn't get a look at his attacker."

"Who just waltzed in and took our evidence! We're destined not to know what was in that bloody thing!" Garrick took several random steps born out of frustration.

"There are two bigger questions," Fanta said. "Bearing in mind that case was down there for months at least, how did the thief know about it? And how did they know the most opportune time to take it?"

"They must've been watching us," said Chib in alarm.

Garrick's mind reeled back to field behind Flanagan's farm, and the man he'd chased. They'd been watched then. Had it ever stopped?

"That meant they knew we were here. Which means they'd followed us," he said.

All three detectives glanced nervously around.

"What about Ian Traynor?" said Garrick. "He was the only one who knew."

"Let's invite him down the station for some questions. Where is he?"

"He was here but went to the hospital with the security guard. He was worried about his legal liability."

Garrick kicked the ground in frustration. This new setback would eat up more resources taking them another step away from the murder itself. Umarov's words came back to mind: *legends grow to shroud facts in the fog of mystery.* That's how Garrick felt; lost in a fog. There was little likelihood of them leaving the office tonight.

"What about security cameras?" he asked, already dreading the answer.

Fanta gave a desperate laugh. "None. We're out in the arse of nowhere. The poor security bloke would've died from exposure if I hadn't turned up with Traynor this afternoon."

"Shit!" Garrick shouted to the sky. It won him a look of

shock from his fellow detectives. He wasn't a man prone to using many profanities, but he couldn't hide his anger. "Whatever all this is about, I bet it was in that case. And now it has disappeared, and let's face it, the chances of it turning up again are almost zero."

Garrick knew the statistics. Despite their best efforts, almost fifty-four per cent of reported crimes went unsolved. Worse, twenty per cent of murders remained unsolved. And with an average of about seven hundred per year, that left one-hundred-forty victims without justice. Or, more chillingly, a possible *one-hundred-forty killers* walking the streets *each year*. He knew the maths, he just didn't want to fall into those same cracks, yet this investigation had the hallmarks of becoming a cold case.

He was now redundant on the site and told Fanta it was best the SOCO team finish their job. He asked her to get a fresh account from the security guard and a statement from Traynor regarding his movements overnight. He and Chib returned to the station.

THE RAIN RETURNED as they silently wound down narrow country roads because the Nissan Leaf's satnav sought to avoid growing congestion on the main Kentish arteries. The silence was broken when Garrick received a call from DC Harry Lord.

"I sent out a couple of feelers regarding Michael Flanagan's death and any business associates he may have had, just as you asked. There was no investigation set up after the crash, despite Kirsty's insistence. The driver of the lorry that hit him was intoxicated and died on impact. Poor sod was the victim of wrong-time, wrong-place. The incident was concluded. A decent life insurance policy paid was out to her, which had been set up years beforehand, and that's around when she stopped insisting there was any wrongdoing."

"So far, so nothing," Garrick grumbled.

"According to Companies House, there was nothing formal set up other than a limited company he ran with Kirsty that seemed to deal with finance for their projects. No audits there. No red flags as far as HMRC are concerned. It was closed after his death."

"Well, it was worth a look." Garrick sighed, wondering why Umarov had dropped in the idea of disgruntled business associates. Was it just out of spite, or to waste their time?

"Hold those horses, Guv." Despite the bad line as they dipped in and out of rural reception, he detected a gleeful edge in Harry's tone. "I asked a few broader questions. And... Quentin... with a..."

The line suddenly dropped out. Garrick's finger tapped the redial icon, but the phone signal was lost.

"You'd think in this day and age we'd have a signal everywhere. Wasn't that the 5G promise? My phone's no quicker than it was in the old fashion 3G days."

When Chib didn't respond, he looked up. She was intently looking between the road ahead and the rear-view mirror. Garrick angled himself to look in the passenger wing mirror. At first, he saw nothing. Then he realised the entire view was taken up by the front grill of a black Range Rover.

A crunching impact came seconds later as the 4x4 ploughed into the back of the Leaf. The crunch of collapsing body panels shattered the silence and the rear window imploded into the car. The impact forcibly jolted Garrick's head back against the seat's headrest.

Chib instinctively mashed the brake with both feet, but

the car was still violently shunted forward at speed. The four electric wheels valiantly tried to grip the wet road, but the inertia was too much. The more powerful Range Rover lunged again as they reached a gentle bend. It was enough of a jolt to cause the Nissan's passenger wheels to slip in a drainage ditch running along the side of the road.

Thick brown water splashed against the windscreen, obliterating the view as the entire world rolled over. Garrick gripped the dashboard as the ground rushed up to meet his side window. Glass exploded close to his ear. The sound of buckling metal filled his world, and he was suddenly upside down, pinned into his seat by the seatbelt, as drainage water rapidly flooded across the inverted roof, and rose towards his scalp.

At the same time, the airbags deployed with a deafening bang, and Garrick was knocked unconscious.

THE TATTOO of rain on the exposed underbelly of the car was all Garrick could hear as he regained consciousness. He was still upside down, the top of his scalp dipped in the cold ditch water that was a couple of inches deep on the roof-cum-floor. It was slowly rising.

His face throbbed, and he winced as he gingerly touched his nose. Trails of blood from it formed thin rivers across his brow and into his hair. As he pushed the slowly deflating airbag away, he noticed his hands were covered in white powder from the airbag's sodium azide propellent. It made his eyes smart. Tears joined the rivulets of blood cascading down his forehead.

Pain burned through his neck as he twisted to look at Chib. She was suspended in her seat too. Her airbag had gone off, and she was unconscious. Blood marred her face, and he wondered if she was in a worse state than him.

"Chib?"

No response. He braced one hand in the cold water to take his weight, then released his seatbelt latch. He inelegantly dropped into the water. With the seat above him, there wasn't much room to right himself. The electrics were shot, so none of the buttons to recline the seat worked. Already the water had risen an inch or two. He was sure the ditch wasn't deep enough to swallow the vehicle, but with all the recent flooding, it was still alarming.

"Hold on, Chib. I'll get you out."

He struggled to manually recline his seat to give him more room to move. The passenger door looked intact, but both side windows had broken and foliage pressing in from the outside. He dropped to his knees to look out of the driver's side windows. The narrow ditch side encroached there too, hemming all four doors closed. A ripple of panic passed through him. They were trapped inside. He murmured assurances to Chib as he processed their situation, although the assurances were more for his own benefit.

His hand went for his pocket to get his phone before he recalled it had jerked from his fingers and bounced around the car when they'd crashed. On his knees, he carefully extended his hands into the murky water to search for it. His fingers touched broken safety glass, a few stones, and some unidentifiable items of detritus before he found it. Hope swelled as he lifted the miraculously glowing screen from the water – only to be replaced by defeat when he saw there was no phone signal.

Both the rear and front windows had shattered, but the Nissan Leaf's sturdy chassis was unbuckled. Fighting the swirling grogginess, and stinging eyes, it took Garrick a few seconds to realise that the car was at an angle, the rear section pressing down a little more than the front. Then he understood. With no conventional engine, the batteries were the heaviest part of the car. From the angle, he judged them to be positioned off-centre and a little more to the rear, but that also explained the water. It wasn't rising, the weight across almost the length of the vehicle was pushing it deeper into the mud.

His suspicion was confirmed moment later when mud suddenly oozed through over the edge of the roof with a loud, wet, sucking noise. His internal panic rose a level. The water may not be deep enough to drown them, but he had no way of judging how deep the mud was.

"Okay, Chib, I'm getting you out. Although it might be a little awkward."

He angled himself as best he could under her, so her head would be cushioned by his belly. Praying she didn't have any spinal injuries, he released her seat belt and was immediately flattened to the floor under her weight. At least he could keep her face out of the water, but for an alarming few moments, he was pinned against the roof. Chib was one of the healthiest members of his team, and he guessed she didn't have an ounce of superfluous fat, but it was still a struggle to position her to sit upright in the water.

"There we go. Piece of cake," he said breathlessly.

The oozing mud was picking up pace as it spread in from the rear window. The car creaked as it sank from the back, raising the bonnet a fraction higher. That was a rare stroke of luck for Garrick.

Hooking both arms under Chib's shoulders, he moved like a crab through the windscreen, falling several times into the muddy water as he hauled his Detective Sergeant out of the vehicle. Once clear of the bonnet, he was able to stand and pull her up the ditch's steep side and back onto the road. He rolled her into the recovery position, checking she wasn't about to swallow her own tongue.

He checked her breathing. It was regular. The pulse on her neck was so strong he could see the vein twitch under her skin. Her nose was broken, and she had small cuts across her face, but as far as he could tell there were no serious lacerations. The little Nissan had protected them well, all things considered.

The heavy rain helped pacify his stinging eyes. The ditch was four feet deep, and just wide enough to pin the door closed. There was no sign of the Range Rover.

Garrick struggled to stay focused as an overwhelming desire to sleep washed over him. He replayed events, but they were short snatches. Over too quickly to provide meaning or detail. He stumbled as he walked to get a better view of the car's rear. It was heavily crumpled from the impact. The more he thought about it, the more certain he was that it wasn't an accident.

They'd been deliberately run off the road.

22

Chib had come around just as a passing vehicle stopped and an elderly man got out to help them. Garrick had sent him away with a phone number direct to his office. It took the man three minutes to find a phone signal, make the call, and return.

The ambulance arrived first, and Garrick sent Chib away in it despite her protests that she was just feeling bruised. He refused to leave, even though the paramedic insisted he needed a scan to check for any fractures. They dabbed his abrasions with something that smarted so much that his eyes wept again.

It was another forty minutes before Fanta arrived, followed by the SOCO team who had been pulled away from the colliery.

Fanta took in Chib's wrecked car. "Wow. I'm so glad it wasn't mine."

He sent her trudging with a forensic officer up the road, searching for debris. They found skid marks and fragments from the Nissan Leaf, but nothing else. The light was dying when the team gave Garrick their initial verdict.

"It was a professional job," a short SOCO officer, with a Brummie accent reported. "From the damage to your car, the Range Rover obviously suffered a few scars too. Broken headlights, fragments of trim, the usual stuff. But there's nothing on the road."

Garrick frowned. "Which means?"

"Somebody took the time to pick it up. Makes it harder to trace." He beckoned Garrick and Fanta to follow him around the front of the Nissan. "It's difficult to tell for sure, but it looks as if a chunk of the windscreen was deliberately pulled free." He indicated a slab of broken glass that was cracked into countless of pieces, but still held together. It lay several feet further from the vehicle. "My guess is that it was tossed aside when somebody clambered in." He looked sideways at Garrick. "How long were you knocked out?"

Garrick shook his head. He didn't recall looking at the time before or after the crash. He could only guess. "Ten minutes, maybe. I think it was the airbag that did it." As he spoke his nose twinged in response.

"Enough time to make a quick search of your car. Is anything missing?"

"You'll have to ask Chib. It's her car. We were not carrying any evidence or anything like that."

"But somebody thought you were," Fanta said, thoughtfully.

Garrick looked curiously at her. "What are you thinking?"

"I'm thinking that you were followed from the mine. Whoever did this thought you might have the case."

Garrick's eyes widened. It was a leap, but it made sense.

"So they attack a pair of detectives to get it back."

"Because they don't know somebody else had stolen it last night."

Garrick ground his teeth as he worked his way through the scenario. The question on his lips faltered as a SOCO officer, knee-deep in the ditch, raised a net she'd been dredging through the water and excitedly called over. The Brummie joined her then returned with something in the palm of his latex glove.

"Does this look familiar?"

"It's an Apple AirTag," Fanta said.

"The question is, does it belong to you or the other detective? Because it was found behind the vehicle. Now it could've been there before, but I bet it fell off the Nissan."

Garrick leaned over to look at the black disc, three centimetres in diameter, with a white edge and the familiar Apple logo in the middle. He was vaguely aware they were generally used by people to track their bags or keys.

"These are a gift to car thieves. There's been a spate of thefts in the area because of these. Thieves see a nice sporty number in the car park, then put the tag discreetly on it so they can track the vehicle later. Find it in the poor bugger's driveway, then nick off with it at their leisure."

Garrick felt an icy grip on his stomach. It was too much of a coincidence to find the AirTag next to the car. Which confirmed they'd been targeted. And if Fanta's theory was valid, then they had *two* conflicting parties involved.

His head swam at the thought. No, not at the thought, it was because he was still concussed. He needed to visit the hospital after all.

. . .

CHIB HAD a broken nose and a rib. She was being kept in for observation overnight. Garrick had a blackeye from where the airbag had struck him, and he'd banged his left wrist hard enough to cause it to swell. Other than more whiplash on top of his previous whiplash, his scans showed nothing else amiss. The doctor had insisted he be kept in for observation too, especially because of his medical history regarding head traumas, but Garrick refused. He knew he'd get a stern tongue lashing from his private physician, Doctor Rajasekar the moment his record was flagged up on her system, but his team couldn't afford to operate with two key officers out of action.

So with cuts cleaned and his wrist bandaged, it was pushing ten o'clock when he was finally discharged and headed home to find Wendy was already asleep and snoring contentedly. His head was throbbing, but sleep failed to claim him. It was three-fifteen in the morning when he checked his phone and saw a message from Molly Meyers asking what had happened. So far, they'd been lucky to avoid any major press involvement, and he wasn't in the mood to do Molly any favours just now.

With Wendy still deeply slumbering, he was kept awake as fragments of the case bounced around his head. Unable to sleep, Garrick got back up and ordered a taxi to the station. He wasn't surprised to find Sean Wilkes asleep at his desk, and Fanta still working, wearing a thick fleece top, zipped up to cover her mouth and nose for warmth. She gave a tired wave that transformed into yawn. Garrick set himself on drinks duty, then joined her at her desk. He passed her a black coffee and cupped his hands around a mint tea as he sat down. They glanced at Wilkes who snorted in his sleep.

"He buckled about half-past one," Fanta said quietly, with a trace of smugness. "No stamina."

Garrick kept his voice to just above a whisper. "The AirTag has been bothering me. Let's assume nobody was in the market to nick a Nissan Leaf. So why tag Chib?"

"Because they know she's on the artefact case."

"The Flanagan case," he corrected her. "A woman has died because of this. So who knows?" He ticked the names off on his fingers. "Mark Cross hasn't met her. Neither has Quentin Morgan. But our two Russian collectors have. She was at Volkov's house and Umarov's yacht. And out of the two of them Umarov was probably at both locations."

"Did you find out what he and Volkov were talking about?"

"Nope. They're obviously rivals, but they both helped the Flanagans discover the mask." Garrick sipped his tea, savouring the warmth in his parched throat. "And Chib had only been to the colliery today, I mean yesterday."

"But that still keeps both of them in the running to tag her car."

"Let's run with that. They tagged her car so they could monitor our investigation. That suggests they were searching for whatever Michael Flanagan had hidden down the mine." Fanta leaned back in her seat and sighed as she put her feet up on the desk. "And they thought we may have found it and taken it with us as evidence."

"That's a little short-sighted when it comes to police procedure. SOCO would have taken it."

"Maybe that's how Russians think? But if any of that is true, then *neither* party took the case."

"Or one did, without the other knowing."

Garrick had blanked that logic step out. He signed. "True. But it leaves open the possibility of a third treasure hunter."

"Liam Brady."

"Which obviously indicates he's alive."

They sat in silence, sipping their drinks and staring into space. The chill in the office was just enough to keep them awake, but now he didn't want it, Garrick felt the claws of slumber reaching for him. His mind was foggy as he tried to slide the pieces of the case around.

"Both Russians had plenty of time getting whatever else the Flanagans found. They shipped everything from the dig to the UK. I'm inclined to think that it's this third-party who beat them, and us, to the mine. And they must have been watching our every move."

He shared his concerns about the figure he'd chased in the field next to Kirsty Flanagan's house and the fact that they must have been followed to the mine when they made the discovery.

Fanta noisily slurped her coffee. "Well, I chased some threads. Firstly, Mark Cross had an alibi last night. He was in a pub quiz. Plenty of witnesses, so he didn't ram you off the road."

"That's mighty thoughtful of him. Did he win?"

"I don't think so. As far as Lord could tell, he doesn't really go to them."

"Then that's quite a convenient alibi."

"The other lead I chased was Umarov. Or rather, the *Perkūnas*." She leaned forward and cycled through several open files until she found a coastal map of Kent. A red path was traced on it. "That's the yacht. It arrived in the UK the day before Kirsty was murdered."

Garrick put his team down and leaned forward for a better look.

"Where did you get this?"

"Boat traffic is tracked, just like airplanes. Vessels are required to have an AIS, an Automatic Identification System, that relays their position, speed, name, usual stuff. It's all run through the Vessel Tracking Service. The *Perkūnas* came in from Monaco, and before that, South Africa."

"And Umarov was onboard?"

"That we can't tell for sure. I checked with Border Force, and he entered the country from that boat, at that time. Whether he was on it at Monaco and South Africa..." she shrugged, *who knows?*

"So he arrives and two days later Kirsty is killed and we're suddenly playing treasure hunt against actors we don't know." He emptied his cup of tea and leaned back in his chair. "What does that tell us?"

They both lapsed into silence again. Garrick hated the opaqueness of each turn they made. It was all shepherding them to one conclusion.

"We must find Liam Brady. Dead or alive, I think he's the key."

Fanta suddenly bolted upright in her chair and slammed her cup down harder than she meant to. The noise made Wilkes snort and shift position in his chair, pulling his coat tighter over him for warmth. DC Liu's fingers clattered across the keyboard as he interrogated the AIS database.

"What?" Garrick asked, but she didn't answer.

She moved at lightning pace, highlighting sections of her notes, and pasting them into search boxes. After a flurry of activity, the AIS system flagged up the *Perkūnas*, this time moored off the coast of Cornwall. She rapped the screen with her knuckle.

"Umarov was here when Michael Flanagan died."

They stared at the green triangle on the map, depicting the super-yacht's position. They were wondering what the odds were that Umarov was in the country both times a Flanagan had died.

"Let's see if Border Force can tell us if Volkov was in the country too," said Garrick. Umarov was inching up their suspect leader board, even if they couldn't fathom a motive. Garrick yawned and closed his eyes. He needed a car, but after trashing the pool car he wasn't sure how many hoops he'd have to jump through for his Super to authorise another. Criminals had it easy. They could just nick one.

GARRICK WOKE WITH A START. His head was on the desk, and a small pool of drool had formed next to his hand. He'd used his swollen wrist as a pillow, and deeply regretted it. He was sure the swelling had increased, and it was now painful to move even a little. Wilkes was no longer at his desk. Fanta was missing, but there were fresh remnants of snacking at her workstation. In the corridor, the ambient buzz of the morning shift was rising. He glanced at his phone. It was just after seven. He stretched, before realising there was a text from an unknown number. That's what must have woken him. It was a simple message: CAR PARK. OUTSIDE. NOW.

Garrick looked around in confusion. His head throbbed, and he wondered if he was having one of his episodes. When the message didn't go away, he decided it best to check out just what was going on.

. . .

THE STATION'S secure car park had a large underground section which Garrick would have preferred to meet in as rain lashed the black tarmac. Instead, he pulled the hood of his Barbour over his uncombed hair and crossed directly to a woman in black jeans and a thick black coat that reached just above her knees. The image of mystery was spoiled by the large red umbrella perched across her shoulder, which she idly rolled back and forth between the fingers of her black leather gloves. It obscured her face until she turned to look at Garrick as he neared. He stopped in surprise.

"Now here's an unexpected twist to my life."

The woman had shoulder length black hair that had a stylish scruffy look cut into it. Her dark eyes widened a little, and a smile smoothed her lupine features.

"David, you say the nicest things."

"Ms Jackson. It still is Ms, isn't it? Or even Jackson?"

The woman gave a little shrug. "Whatever name suits."

Garrick had briefly met the woman who claimed to be from Military Intelligence. Her real name, and even her job, was shrouded in secrecy. Only her association with the MET's DCI Oliver Kane gave her a stamp of authenticity. Yet, behind the scenes, he knew she was connected at the highest levels. The only time they had crossed paths to help one another was to expose the tendrils of the Murder Club, which had its origins in the Falklands Conflict

The atmosphere of clandestine subterfuge was ruined by their need to speak loudly over the rain drumming against the umbrella and his hood, and the occasional staff members arriving and nodding a greeting to Garrick.

"Imagine my surprise when your name crossed my path again," she continued.

"That makes one of us surprised, and one of us

confused."

"Then I'll cut to the chase. Black market antiquities are big business. Up there with poaching, human trafficking and drugs for making people rich. The Flanagans are, were, on our watch list, so their deaths raised antenna."

"They were involved in the black market?"

"They were fringe players. I can't say we have any direct proof they willingly did so, but I don't need to tell you that lack of proof doesn't equal innocence."

"I don't know if I can help you on that. We're running around in circles at the moment."

"I know. Losing evidence when its right under your nose." Her disapproval irritated Garrick.

"Evidence I was a step ahead of you guys from finding," he said with a smirk.

Jackson gave a dismissive sniff. "Nevertheless, I feel it's crucial to us both, to find the contents of that case." As Garrick was about to reply, she pressed on. "And we're familiar with the Russians, but any intel you can furnish us with will be useful. They've been tough nuts to crack."

"They could also be innocent collectors."

She smiled. "Ah, David. That's what I like about you." He waited to hear exactly what that was, but her eyes shot around the car park before settling on him like an attractive predator. "Your missing Liam Brady, any joy there?"

"You eloquently summed it up with the word 'missing'," he deadpanned. "But I suppose you're going to give me a file that opens up the entire can of worms."

She gave a husky laugh. "Really? If we had that, then we'd quietly act upon it. That's what we do. We don't meet in car parks and solve everybody else's cases. You must really think about the nature of our relationship."

Garrick gave it a few seconds thought. He smiled, although he didn't like the answer. "I'm under-resourced, under pressure, and yet I'm your last hope to make a break-through."

She tried unsuccessful to snap her gloved fingers. "Got it in one. You're my desperate chance card." She tilted her head as she gauged his reaction. "It's sweet that you don't realise how much of a compliment that is. Maybe I know how you think better than you do. You're casting far and wide for clues, when invariably the answers are right in front of you."

"Ooh, cryptic. My favourite unhelpful thing."

Jackson sighed, indicating the conversation was at an end. "Well, there it is. I can help you free up some limited resources with a little help from above." She nodded her head towards an old Volkswagen Polo she'd been leaning against. It was one of the pool cars what was on its way out. "Can't have you saving the day in a taxi, can we?" She turned to leave, heading to an average looking black Hyundai i40 Saloon blocking in several other vehicles. "One last thing. Be careful. You may think antiques are not dangerous. But the players are very dangerous people. The little incident with DS Okon's car last night; think of it as a polite enquiry."

BACK IN THE INCIDENT ROOM, Fanta and Wilkes had returned from the canteen. They looked tired, but still enthusiastic. DC Harry Lord entered, carrying three steaming coffees. He was sniffling, and his red nose indicated his cold was getting worse.

"Oh, morning, Guv. Didn't know you were in yet." Garrick scowled but didn't pass comment. Lord handed the coffees to the other two constables. "The DS called in. They're discharging her later, but she's feeling pretty banged up."

"She needs to stay at home."

"Yeah. She's trying to work out what to do about her wedding."

Garrick blinked in surprise. He'd completely forgot about that. It was this weekend.

Sneezing, Lord continued as he returned to his desk. He sounded blocked up when he spoke. "I know me missus would be cancel everything rather than have her big day look like a car crash. Literally, in Chib's case."

Garrick stood in front of the evidence wall and soaked everything in. The maps, the photos, the names, the network of arrows and abundance of question marks. Was Jackson correct that they had everything right here? What were they missing?

Wilkes scrolled through his emails. "Forensics confirm the skid marks at the crash site were from a Range Rover. Nothing you didn't know. They estimate it was doing forty-five when it shunted you off the road."

"Any such vehicles registered with the Russians?"

"Already checked. They're not so stupid to do that."

Garrick cast his eyes over the photos of the crime scene in Kirsty's kitchen. The killer was looking for something, something she died to protect. In this case, the tracker that eventually led to the flight case in the mine.

The case's subsequent theft indicates there were at least two parties searching for it.

Back to basics.

He took a closer look at the photos Fanta had taken of the maps and printouts pinned to the wall in Brady's rented house. One of them indicated Kirsty's home. Was that because a clue had led him there, or he already knew where she lived?

Then there were the Russians who financed the Flanagans' last great find, and the stuffy museum curator who successfully outbid them for it.

There was Mark Cross, the security guard who found Kirsty's body. An innocent bystander in all of this... if it wasn't for his odd discrepancies regarding how many times he'd met Kirsty Flanagan. Once officially, twice according to Cross.

Then there was Ian Traynor, the civil servant who was the only other person who knew about their discovery in the colliery just before it was stolen.

Finally, Michael Flanagan who died in an accident while trying to orchestrate the sale of the rare Neolithic mask they'd found. The term 'accident' was tasting sour the more Garrick scrutinised it.

His eyes flittered back and forth, hoping something would jump out rather than a bunch of arrows and question marks. In some cases, Fanta had punctuated words with three question marks to vent her frustration. He was aware the others were talking across the office as they shared updates, but Garrick filtered them out. If Military Intelligence were looking into aspects of the case and had hit a dead end, then what hope did they have?

He was drawn back to the photos Fanta had taken of the papers Brady had pinned to his wall. He leaned closer, squinting to make details out, but the printouts were poor quality.

"Liu, let me see the pictures you took at the house."

The sharp use of her surname cut the witty retort she was about to throw back. Instead, she accessed the folder and opened each of the high-resolution pictures. Garrick took the mouse from her and cycled through them, stopping at the map depicting Kirsty Flanagan's house, with the roads highlighted. He used his finger to indicate each item.

"Kirsty's house. The highlighted roads, the way he'd zoomed in on the area, indicates to me he was unfamiliar with it. Maybe hadn't been there before. If he had, why show any detail? Unless he was staking it out. Looking for the best exit points."

Fanta nodded, unsure where her boss was heading. Garrick scrolled to another map pinned to the wall. This was a wider representation of Kent, with an X marked on it. He circled the mouse pointer over it.

"Whereas this isn't detailed. So why mark it up?"

Fanta shrugged. "I looked it up. It's between Ash, where Flanagan lived, and Sandwich."

"Show me."

Fanta took the mouse from his hand and slid the keyboard nearer. She opened Google Maps and zoomed in on the approximate area.

"There you are. If anything's buried around there, we're not going to find it."

Garrick took the mouse and zoomed in, moving a few miles south until a village appeared between the two others.

"But there's *that*." Fanta pulled a face. She didn't get it. Garrick spoke up to address the rest of the room. "Does Woodnesborough mean anything?"

Lord didn't take his eyes off his emails as he replied. "Yeah, Guv. It's where Mark Cross lives."

Garrick grinned as he turned to Fanta. He tapped the screen.

"This isn't X-marks the spot. It's Mark *Cross*. He and Brady know each other!"

23

D C Fanta Liu usually enjoyed a good stakeout, but this time she was uncharacteristically subdued. Maybe it was because of experience. Sitting in wait with her boss had led to bad things before. In one case, it had almost killed her, and she still bore the scars from triggering an explosive device. Or perhaps it was Garrick's own nervousness projecting onto her? The violent attack on him and Chib indicated the perps had no issues with knocking people out of their way – civilians or cops.

They'd parked Garrick's Polo, which his Super had signed off without comment, or even being asked to do so. He just gave a hard stare as he passed the authorisation to Garrick. It was a perfectly crappy car to blend in.

Woodnesborough was a quaint Kentish village, built around the 13th century Anglican church of St Mary the Blessed Virgin. They'd parked on the corner of the imaginatively named main thoroughfare, *The Street*, so they could see into the branching Elmwood Park new build estate where Mike Cross had bought a house. *Bought* being the unusual word, especially on his salary. A two-year-old Volkswagen Beetle was parked outside a terrace house with a bright yellow door. The layer of dark mud and grime coating the vehicle's sides made Garrick think it was grey, but glimmers of white were speckled across the roof.

After going through the gauntlet of selling his own house, Garrick was savvy enough to know the true price of home ownership.

"How much do you think he paid for that? New build, so I doubt it was inherited. Unmarried. According to the electoral register, he lives alone."

"His office confirmed he's taken the week off," said Fanta. "Flu, he said."

They lapsed into silence and watched nothing happen in the street. After fifteen minutes, Fanta stretched in her seat.

"Are you sure this is a good use of our time?" she ventured.

"Absolutely not. But we've got little to go on."

"Well... he could really have the flu. Which means we could be here for days."

"What do you want to do? Knock on his door and offer him some chicken soup?"

"Why not? How else are we going to question him?"

"He's been evasive at the best of times. Why would he change now?"

The front door suddenly opened, and Mark Cross stepped out in a padded jacket and tossed some boxes into the green wheelie bin next to the door before thumbing his car alarm off and getting in. Seconds later he drove quickly past Garrick and Fanta without a glance. They tried to crouch in their seats, but Cross was driving at such a pace he didn't slow down to take notice.

"He looked fit enough to me," said Garrick, opening his door and climbing out.

"What are you doing?" Fanta asked, as she followed him.

"What's the point in watching an empty house?"

Double-checking the Beetle had disappeared around the far bend, Garrick walked up the footpath and opened the green recycle bin. It was filled with takeout cartons and pizza boxes.

"Quite a healthy appetite," he commented as Fanta caught him up. "Looks as if he's eating for two."

He peered through the front window, cupping his hands around his eyes to see inside. He reacted to a sudden movement as a figure darted out of the room.

"Somebody's home," he murmured. "Ring the bell."

Fanta did so before realising it was a Ring video doorbell. The sort that could be answered on a mobile phone from anywhere in the world. She shot an alarmed look at Garrick as they heard the chime inside the house, but nobody answered. Seconds passed before Cross's voice issued from the speaker.

"Yes?"

Fanta couldn't run, she had to play it out. "Mark Cross? I'm DC Liu from Kent Police, I'd like to ask you a few questions."

"I'm not home. You'll have to arrange something with my solicitor."

"It won't take long," Fanta pressed. "Perhaps I can talk to whoever's at home right now?"

There was a long pause, and she wondered if they'd been cut off. Then:

"There's nobody home. Speak to my solicitor."

Then silence once more. She looked at Garrick who

hadn't moved from the window. He reached across and covered the camera with his hand. When Fanta was about to speak, he put a finger on his lips and nodded to the lawn. Fanta frowned, forcing him into pantomime mouthing, *"use the dirt!"* Then he nodded at the doorbell.

Fanta gave an "oh!" of understanding. She knelt to scoop up a palm of wet mud, then pressed it over the doorbell camera as Garrick removed his hand. It stayed in place, obscuring the lens. Satisfied, he darted back to the window and knocked on the glass. He was about to bark an order to Fanta, then remembered the doorbell's microphone still worked. Instead he mimed – *you stay here, I'm going around the back.*

He darted to the left cutting across the front gardens of several other houses before reaching the end of the terrace where the road continued down to a car park outside the village hall. His whiplash injuries stabbed like needles through his limbs and took his breath away.

There was nothing but a large field behind the line of homes, each with a narrow back garden of their own. He started counting the buildings to identify which was Cross's – but stopped when he saw a man scrambling over a fence to make his escape. He spotted Garrick and immediately dropped back into the garden and returned into the house.

Garrick hesitated. "Crap!" he didn't have the energy to run back and forth all day. But he had to warn Fanta. Sucking in a deep breath, he sprinted the way he came.

Once again, he rounded the corner onto the driveway in time to see the man racing from the house, towards the hedge blocking the main road. Fanta was sprawled on the floor. The front door had been left open, and Fanta was already picking herself up to give chase.

"Stop! Police! You bastard!" she yelled in pain.

The man shouldered through the hedge and was on the main road before she could stand. At the end of the driveway, Garrick had the advantage of keeping on the road as he ran onto The Street. His target was already fifty yards ahead and gave no signs of slowing.

"Police!" he yelled, although it came out as not much more than a wheeze.

By the time he built up speed, Fanta shouldered through the hedge, through the ragged gap that had already been created. DC Liu was quicker on her feet and sped up as their target reached a Y-shaped fork in the road. He veered to the right and Garrick could tell he was already slowing down.

There was a bellow of horsepower ahead of them – and a black Range Rover screamed down the street directly towards the fleeing man. He tried to dart aside, but not before it clipped him. Garrick stumbled to a halt as the man was flipped in the air and rolled across the vehicle's bonnet. He struck the windshield, starring the glass.

It didn't stop.

Fanta jumped into the ditch to the left, but from the angle Garrick was standing, he couldn't judge if she'd been hit or not. He didn't have time to think as the Range Rover, with the man still on the bonnet, sped straight at him.

Garrick threw himself to the right. A bad choice as there was no ditch to save him, but a raised embankment. He pressed himself flat and felt the violent rush of wind as the car zipped past. He caught glimpses of a broken headlight and crumpled bumper. He was certain it was the same one that had rammed him off the road.

Then he felt himself sucked towards the car. It passed just before he could collide with it, and he tumbled into the street, coughing on the cloud of grey petrol fumes. By the time he looked up, the car had disappeared around the bend. He wobbled as he stood up.

"Fanta!"

Turning, he dreaded what he'd find. Fortunately, it was a furious Detective Constable pulling herself out of a flooded ditch. Her clothes were dripping with mud, and as she lifted both arms, Garrick couldn't shake the image of Bigfoot out of his mind.

24

The police chopper arrived on the scene before any support vehicles could make it. Between Garrick and Fanta they had pieced together the Range Rover's registration plate, and an alert had been put out to apprehend Mark Cross.

Garrick was unsure whether they had witnessed a hit-and-run or a kidnapping. Fanta confirmed the runner was Liam Brady. She'd got up-close and personal when he opened the front door and punched her in the face. At least with the front door left open, they had no legal issues preventing them from entering the house. The bigger problem was keeping the growing cloud of gawking neighbours away before they trampled any evidence. Once uniformed officers arrived, Garrick and Fanta had space to explore Cross's home.

Everything was new. The kitchen, the leather sofa, and the huge TV bolted to the wall.

"Somebody has been on a spending spree," Fanta noted as she dripped mud across the new beige carpet.

The spare bedroom had been slept in, presumably by Brady. A mix of freshly laundered clothes and crumbled worn items were scattered around the room. They decided not to search it until forensics had been through everything.

The kitchen's back door was still open. Garrick indicated a pair of chunky orange heavy-duty torches. The sort ideal for exploring tunnels deep underground. However, hopes of finding the stolen flight case were quickly scotched.

WITH A DUAL SEARCH underway for Mark Cross and the Range Rover, things started moving with a sense of urgency that had been so far lacking in the investigation. For several hours, Garrick felt at a loose end as everybody else chased leads, while he waited on results. He'd wanted to visit Chib at home, but now that wouldn't happen. Instead, he FaceTimed her.

She was at home, wrapped in fleecy green pyjamas. Several prominent white stitches on her cheeks and forehead stood out against her dark skin. Her nose was still swollen as was the skin under her right eye, which was livid red.

"You look great," he said with a wry smile.

"Wedding ready," she replied with a sigh.

"About that. I'm sorry Chib... I..."

"Sorry for what? It happened to us both. Just the job, I supposed."

"It is the way we do it. Do you think other detectives experience the same bad luck we do?" She gave a small smile in response and switched rooms so she could sit down. Garrick caught a fleeting glimpse of her home and was reminded just how little he knew about his team's personal lives. "So what's the plan for the weekend?"

"We're going to postpone the wedding." She indicated her face. "It would cost far too much to Photoshop this mess. Some of the family in Nigeria are going to reschedule, but I think it'll end up being a much smaller affair. That's probably a good thing." She was upset but hid it as she cleared her throat. "Anyway, I'm going to be in tomorrow–"

"No chance. Let's see how you feel next week. Besides, I think we may have everything wrapped up by the end of the day. So other than relieve Harry on the coffee run, there'll be nothing for you to do."

She raised a sceptical eyebrow. "Really, Guv? You're forgetting this is a video call. I can see you too. And you look like shit."

Garrick burst into laughter at the unexpected insult. He caught his image on the phone's front-facing camera. His face was streaked with mud, and his hair looked wild.

He smirked. "Busted."

Wilkes excitedly waved at him from across the office.

"Mark Cross is in custody!"

Garrick gave him a thumbs-up, and the call with Chib came to a swift end. Before he could cross to Wilkes, Harry Lord intercepted him.

"The chopper found the Range Rover. It's on fire in the middle of nowhere. No sign of any passengers. It's going to be gutted by the time the fire service reaches it."

"Can they hover in low? Fan the flames out?"

"Too dangerous, apparently." Harry's eyebrows bobbed to suggest that if he was flying, that's exactly what would have happened. "We ran the plate. It's owned by a knitting company based in Warwickshire."

"Another shell company." Harry nodded and suddenly

looked uneasy. "What is it? You have the look of someone bearing bad news."

"Fanta was bothered by the timing of the Range Rover turning up."

"Me too. There was no way they could've known where we were going."

"And I think you would've noticed if you were being followed..."

"Another AirTag?"

Harry looked too embarrassed to answer. His gaze slid over to Fanta who had entered the office in fresh clothes. She wore a slightly oversized light grey hooded fleece, which he was sure he'd seen Wilkes wearing, faded blue jeans and white trainers. She hadn't had time to go home, so he guessed Wilkes had fetched them. She had snatched a shower in the changing room; something Garrick should do with himself. In her hand she held what looked like a small thick-handled electric fly swatter.

"Strip search, boss!"

Garrick heard Harry snigger, but he forced a straight face. Now she was closer, he could see the device looked more like the handheld metal detectors used in airport security. Fanta swished the device as if it was a sword.

"I borrowed a bug detector from surveillance. I've already done my clothes before I set them on fire. Now it's your turn."

She thumbed switch, and an LED came to life. She edged it towards Garrick and immediately the device emitted a whine. Garrick looked at her in alarm.

"Hands up and spread 'em," she said in a cod-American accent.

Garrick extended his arms to his sides and Fanta ran the scanner over the top and underside of his sleeves. The whine remained a constant pitch. She moved it down, across his chest, to his belt buckle.

"Turn around."

Garrick did so, and she swept it over his shoulders, then his butt and down the back of his legs. The tone remained the same. He turned back so she could wave the wand over his groin, shins, and then she finally crouched as he lifted his feet so she could pass over his soles. Again, the tone remained the same.

"Mmm?" She looked at the settings on the device.

Lord reached for it. "Are you sure you're using it right?"

Fanta moved it from his reach. "Ah, ah." The tone remained the same. Curious, she stepped back from her boss. As she moved the probe closer to Harry's head, the whine continued.

"Well, we know there's nothing in there." She held it at arm's length and slowly turned in a circle. The tone rose slightly. She froze. Then walk forward, the noise rose in pitch with each step. Finally she stopped at Garrick's desk and dramatically lowered the probe over his Barbour. The tone shot up. "Um, boss...?"

Garrick shot over and yanked his jacket from the back of his chair. Holding it by the shoulders, he lifted it so Fanta could slowly move the scanner over the fabric. It peaked above the hem. Garrick pinched his fingers along the cloth, searching. Then he felt something. He laid the jacket flat on a desk and used his fingers to locate a small bump hidden inside the lining.

"I need a knife."

Harry disappeared to his desk and returned with a Victorinox Swiss Army Knife. Garrick opened the small blade and looked closer. There was a small hole punctured into the waxed cotton hem. He used the blade to widen it, conscious not to ruin his jacket. Then he guided the object out with his thumbnail.

It was a pointed tube the length of his thumb and half a centimetre in diameter. He tossed his jacket to Harry, and Fanta scanned it again. The tone was weak, only rising when she moved the detector over the device.

"That looks like a serious piece of kit," said Harry. "When did you pick that up?"

Garrick slowly shook his head, before it occurred to him.

"The crash. They used the AirTag to track the car. When they searched the vehicle, they must've planted this on me then." He looked at Fanta in alarm. "Go to Chib's place and check her out."

Fanta silently nodded, and headed straight out, pausing only to snatch her canvas jacket from her chair. "Fanta, check everybody out. And the cars."

She stopped and stabbed the detector at Harry.

"Spread 'em."

Harry obliged as she circled him, moving the device slowly up and down.

Garrick's eyes didn't leave the tracker in the palm of his hand. "How 'serious' would you say this is?"

"I wouldn't be surprised if it was military grade."

Garrick harrumphed. They weren't the words he wanted to hear.

25

There were not enough forensic technicians or free lab-space available in the county to look at all the separate crime scenes blossoming like a bad acne outbreak. The situation was made more difficult because Garrick couldn't get hold of additional resources and was doing his utmost to make sure Chib recovered at home.

Fanta had found another tracking device planted in the sole of the boots Chib had worn during the crash. They'd been confirmed as high-end devices of military origin which were not available to the average stalker.

Lord and Wilkes were stretched but doing an admirable job at overseeing the search at Mark Cross's property and delving deeper into his background. None of this had a positive effect on Garrick's mood when he paid Mark Cross a visit in the interview room.

The security guard calming sat with the same solicitor as they all waited for the recording device to spin up to speed. Garrick did they usual introductory notes, then fixed a scowl on Cross.

"Harbouring a wanted felon is a criminal offence." He tapped his pen on the notes in front of him.

"My client wasn't aware Mr Brady was wanted by the police. You'd never told him this, for one."

Cross nodded in agreement.

"Forensics are combing through your house right now. They're looking particularly closely at Brady's clothing. Do you think they're likely to find traces of blood?"

Cross cleared his throat. "How would I know?"

"Because they were laundered at your house."

Did Garrick detect a slight stiffening of Cross's posture, or was that just wishful thinking?

"Were you aware of his intentions the night Kirsty Flanagan was murdered?"

The solicitor raised his hand. "My client has already stated where he was working that night. It's on record."

"That's not what I asked," Garrick snapped back. The patience he normally reserved for interviews was depleted through stress and lack of sleep.

"No comment," Cross shot back.

The solicitor rolled his eyes and motioned to his client to shut up. That gave Garrick assurance that Cross was on the ropes.

Garrick decided to hit him from multiple angles. Confusion usually made people slip up as they tried to keep up with the layers of conflicting lies they were weaving.

"Do you want to tell me how a man on your salary lives the lifestyle you do?"

"I... it's my money..." Cross said weakly.

"And I'm greatly looking forward to learning about how you got it." He paused long enough for Cross to open his mouth to respond – but Garrick cut him off.

"How long have you known Mr Brady?"

Cross blinked, already on the back foot. "About four years. We'd worked together on the ferries."

"And you told him how to bypass Kirsty Flanagan's home security?" It was a guess, but Garrick delivered it as Gospel fact.

Cross stuttered. "He wanted to know how security systems worked..."

Garrick suspected the man would clam up in a torrent of '*no comments*' if he delved further. It was better to keep dancing around. Keep him unbalanced.

"What did you do with the case you retrieved from the mine?"

Cross mouthed like a goldfish and looked to his solicitor for help. His legal rep was diligently making notes on the conversation so didn't see.

"I don't..." Cross stuttered. "I had nothing to do with Kirsty's death. He said he didn't do that."

"Aiding and abetting a murder is an offense."

"How, if I didn't know?"

The dominos in Garrick's mind were toppling. He made a few abbreviated notes on the printout in front of him, linking them together with arrows to make sure the chronology made sense. The silence gave more time for Mark Cross to stew. He was now sweating and lightly scratching the table with his nails.

Garrick let the magic of silence apply its own pressure. Cross licked his lips.

"He paid me for details on the security system. He wanted to talk to her after Michael's death, but she was avoiding him. What was he supposed to do?"

"What did he tell you she owed him?" Garrick was taking

another punt, so he framed the question as vaguely as possible.

Cross gave a dismissive laugh. "Everything he was promised!"

Garrick was determined not to admit his ignorance. "And how much were you promised?"

"Half a mil." Cross hung his head. "But I didn't know anybody would be hurt."

"What did Brady tell you about his business relationship with the Flanagans?"

"Michael?" Garrick made a mental note that he'd pointedly detached Kirsty, implying she wasn't aware of the deal. Cross rocked side to side on the hard interview seat. "He was Michael's negotiator. Without him..."

"You are aware Michael was killed in a traffic accident."

"Assassinated." Cross said it with conviction.

"By whom?"

Cross shrugged. "It was a warning for us to be careful."

Garrick decided it was worth another gamble. "We tried to apprehend Brady at your house, but he ran." He noted the look of relief on Cross's face. "He was struck by a car, then kidnapped." Garrick hated the rush of *schadenfreude* he felt. "You'd be helping him if you told me where you think he is."

Mark Cross stared back at him for a long time.

"HE'S FRIGHTENED FOR HIS LIFE." Garrick walked from the interview room in a great deal of pain. The soft tissue damage ached his back and neck, and his wrist was itching beneath the bandage. Because of the lack of sleep, he felt as if he was running on fumes. But with a possible active kidnapping situation he couldn't go home.

Neither would Mark Cross. He'd was being kept for twenty-four hours so they could piece together the appropriate charges from his confession so far. What they needed was more information about Liam Brady's relationship with Michael Flanagan. Lord kept pace with Garrick as they pushed through a fire door in the corridor leading to the canteen. Garrick's stomach was rumbling with anticipation.

"My money's on the Russians," said Lord as he blew his nose. He wasn't in a fit state to keep working, but Garrick couldn't afford to lose him. "That's pretty obvious."

"Question is which one?"

"Let's arrest them both. They're rich. They've got to be guilty of *something*. There was nothing useful found at the burned out Range Rover. The fire had extinguished itself by the time the firefighters got there. Whoever did it used an accelerant to get the job done. There were a few cottages around, so uniform went door-to-door, but nobody saw anything. The chopper ran various routes between the wreck and Woodnesborough, using thermals to search for Brady's body, but found nothing."

Although it wasn't absolute confirmation, it strengthened the argument that Liam Brady had been kidnapped and striking him with the car had been an accident. Garrick replayed the scene. He had led the kidnappers to Brady through the tracker planted on him. Like him, the kidnappers had probably hoped to find the missing flight case at the house but with the police present, they had taken Brady instead. Which begged the question, what had they intended to do it if he and Fanta had got to the man first?

From the pattern of blunt violence, he could only conclude they have used force. He had to remind himself that they'd kidnapped Kirsty Flanagan's *murderer*, or potential murderer. In the hierarchy of ruthlessness, Garrick was wondering where the kidnappers sat.

He put that aside for now. The question of what precious treasure was worth killing for, was the next issue. If Brady had promised to give Mark Cross half a million quid for helping him, just how much was he expecting to make? Or did he intend to kill Cross afterwards to ensure his silence?

"Sean had a thought," Lord said as they entered the canteen. The smell of baked potatoes struck Garrick's nostrils and made his stomach rumble again. They took a tray and joined the queue of staff waiting to be served. "Brady thinks Michael Flanagan was assassinated. That suggests Brady's doing this out of revenge."

"Maybe. But he's definitely doing it for the cash." They shuffled forward as the line in front slowly whittled down. "Problem with that idea is, how could it be revenge if he then killed Michael's wife?"

"Yeah," Lord said thoughtfully as he placed his tray on the counter and started sliding it past the healthy salad options and towards the jacket potatoes and baked beans.

Sean Wilkes entered the canteen, his head pivoting around searching for them. He spotted the taller Harry Lord and darted over.

"Guv! Got something," he said breathlessly.

Garrick's hand hovered over the stack of clean plates as he waited for Wilkes to get on with it.

Wilkes was grinning with delight. "It's always something small, right? Just a detail that–"

"Sean. Tell me before I starve to death," Garrick snapped.

"Mark Cross's licence plate came up on the London Congestion charge system the morning *after* the case was whizzed from the mine. Seven-oh-eight, to be exact."

"So he has an alibi?"

Sean shook his head. "I don't think so. I think he messed up. If he was nine minutes earlier, he wouldn't have had to pay. He slipped up with his timing, I bet because he was driving in from the colliery."

Garrick tried to ignore the impatient sighs coming from the others behind him in the queue.

Sean smiled. "We've got the photo from the traffic camera. It's Cross alright. And Liam Brady is in the passenger seat."

"Where were they going?"

Sean's smile widened. "Through the magic of ANPR, I can tell you they parked at the NCP in Bloomsbury Square for forty-seven minutes."

"Bloomsbury Square?" Garrick's London geography was limited, but it rang a bell. "Isn't that close to the museum?"

"Literally around the corner."

Garrick left his tray on the counter and stepped out of the line. Food would have to wait.

26

There was no time to get a search warrant, and David Garrick had to admit that the evidence was too flimsy to do so. He was also operating under the auspices of another police force. Whilst it technically shouldn't be a problem, it could cause complications down the line. And he didn't have the staff to spare. If they didn't build up coherent charges against Mark Cross, then his solicitor would have him free by tomorrow and Garrick was worried the man was a flight risk. He needed Harry Lord to focus on that. Fanta was pushing every lever they had to track down their kidnapped murderer, and he needed Sean Wilkes to keep digging into this new seam of information.

He had little choice but to call Chib and beg her to come to the office. To her credit, she needed little persuasion. Rearranging the wedding was annoying her, so work was a welcome break. Garrick would have preferred her to come with him to the museum as backup but sensed there would be political problems if he forced an injured colleague to the frontline.

Instead, he drove into London alone. He stopped by the staff canteen to make himself a black coffee, something he had avoided for a long time. It played havoc with his stomach, and as he hadn't eaten, it would probably be crippling. He also knew the caffeine would wire him up for the rest of the day. It certainly drove him to make questionable decisions, such as calling up the London MET for help.

In particular, one man he had little love for.

"DCI Kane," came the clipped voice over Garrick's wired hands-free headphones. His phone had slipped between his seat and the middle console when he dialled Kane's number. It would have to stay there until he could fish it out by pulling the wire. Something he didn't want to risk as the last time that happened, the headphones had unplugged, leaving the phone stranded.

"Oliver, it's David Garrick."

"Garrick! Good Lord. What's the matter, did you butt-dial me by mistake?"

After his past encounters with Kane, hearing him joke felt unnatural. Kane had been the MET detective investigating elements of the Murder Club, which led him to David Garrick, who had been friends with John Howard, who turned out to be the chief architect of the murderous cabal. When his sister had fallen prey to them, Garrick had been placed high on the suspect list. It had been an arduous time, which saw DS Chibarameze Okon inserted into his team. And now Garrick was asking the same man for help.

He outlined the case as quickly as he could, highlighting the visit from their mutual acquaintance, Ms Jackson. He hoped the Military Intelligence angle would spike Kane's cooperation.

"Of course, we can't just bluster into the museum and

start searching it. Even if we had a warrant, a search could take weeks. Months. And if the case has been emptied, we don't know what we're looking for."

Garrick gave a weary sigh as he turned onto the M26, pushing just under eighty miles per hour.

"I know, and I'm not asking you to do anything. I just thought having you along may spook him enough."

"Knowing you, it feels as if you're asking me to do something that's not strictly by the book."

"You know me..." Garrick said, which was more of a brutal admission than a simple 'yes'.

To his surprise, Kane laughed.

"You really are something. First you poach one of my best detective sergeants, then you try to coerce me into some foolish attempt to break into the British Museum." There was a long pause. Garrick thought he'd hung up. Then: "I'll meet you there."

GETTING into the museum was straightforward once the grumpy security guard had taken time to assess their IDs. Flashing the MET and Kent Constabulary cards had given him pause for thought, and he made a quick call to verify DCI Kane's authenticity before letting them through. Garrick would ordinarily approve such pedantic behaviour, but it was late afternoon, and he was fatigued and aching all over.

Once through, tracking down any staff felt more like a game. As soon as they were approached, the staff quickly scuttled away on urgent business. Garrick eventually cornered one young academic, who looked so punky it was if she was desperately defying stereotypes. She'd seen Quentin Morgan leaving about two o'clock. Garrick assured her he'd return for their appointment, and she obligingly used her ID card to let them pass into the restricted area.

"That was too easy," Garrick observed as he got his bearings and headed towards Quentin Morgan's office.

"I think I should recommend a security overhaul here," Kane muttered, shaking his head. "Disgraceful."

After two wrong turns in the labyrinthine passageways, they were put on the right track by a tall thin man who was trying to read a report as he walked. Then they were in the storage area that doubled as Quentin Morgan's office. Kane examined the range of artefacts on the open shelves. Presumably all worth a fortune and left lying around.

"How much did he pay for that mask?" he asked incredulously.

Garrick headed straight for his desk. The computer was on, a screen saver cycled through pictures of exotic white sand beaches. He waggled the mouse, and the desktop appeared without a password prompt.

"He left in a hurry..." he muttered.

He felt a growing sense of unease and couldn't put his finger on what was bothering him. He looked around the room for the case.

"Look for a silver flight case, this big." He indicated the dimensions with his hands.

There were plenty of cardboard boxes, a few stamped with the Amazon logo, others with shipping numbers printed across them. There was even an old wooden crate filled with dry straw, but no flight case. Garrick ruffled through the straw, just to be sure.

Kane shook his head and sat at the desk. "This is the problem, searching for something when we don't know what it is." He pointed to a crude stone triangle on the shelf next to him. "For all we know it could be this."

"That's an axe head," Garrick said after a quick glance.

"Did he have an assistant? Somebody who could tell us if something new has turned up?"

Garrick pulled two of the nearest deep drawers open and glanced inside. "Not that I know of. What about his computer?" Kane put his hand on the mouse and stared at the computer desktop but didn't make any move to open any application. "What's the matter? Surely you know how to use a computer?"

"I'm just trying to work out how many rules I'm violating." He caught Garrick's disapproving expression. "He's not missing, you have no warrant, he doesn't have a legal rep present–"

Garrick knocked Kane's hand aside and used the mouse to access the curator's emails.

"It's amazing you actually make any arrests," he muttered.

Kane rose from the seat so Garrick could sit.

Three unread emails at the top of the stack appeared to be from other academics. Two more were spam. The last one marked as 'read' was from a string of five numbers, with no name assigned to it. Garrick frowned. The obvious spam emails below it had all been left unread, which indicated Quentin wasn't in the habit of opening any old junk. Garrick clicked it.

It was one line: HELIPORT. NOW.

"What time did that woman say he left?"

Kane was leaning over a shelf, examining a rock carving of some sort. "About two."

The email was time stamped one-fifty-four.

"Where's the nearest heliport?"

"Heliport? I don't know. City Airport, probably. Why?"

Garrick could kick himself for not asking the punk-academic if Quentin had the case. They could ask to see security footage, but that would take time. Already, the curator had a two-hour lead on them.

"He left quickly. And I know of one particular place he'd take a helicopter to."

Garrick felt a cold chill run through him. What danger was the bumbling academic about to walk into?

27

There was no time left. Garrick had the acute sense that no matter what he did, it would be too late.

He knew also that he was acting on the flimsiest of evidence back by nothing more than a hunch. If he was wrong, his rash actions could cost him his career.

A few calls from DCI Kane put the MET's more substantial resources in action. It took ten minutes to confirm that a private Bell 505 Jet Ranger X helicopter had taken off from London City Airport, bound for Kent.

Garrick ran, or at least briskly jogged, to his car in the same NCP car park Mark Cross had used. He set the satnav and headed to Ramsgate with the siren blazing and the blue light on the dash blinking.

With his team nearer, Harry Lord was dispatched to Ramsgate Royal Harbour and Marina to confirm Garrick's suspicion. He'd just made it through heavy Surrey traffic, and onto the M25 by the time Lord arrived and confirmed the same helicopter was indeed on the helipad of Bilol Umarov's super-yacht.

Garrick tried to call his Superintendent but kept getting his voicemail. Instead, he rang Chib at the office and told her to interrupt their Super so he could allow them to board the ship.

As he pulled back onto the M26 at a sub-legal speed because of congestion, Chib called him back.

"Guv, the Super's having none of it. He wants a written report, with the evidence carefully laid out."

"You told him we don't have time? If Quentin Morgan has taken the flight case onboard, then there is no telling what they may do to him. They have attacked us, and people have been killed for what's inside it."

"And unless we know what that is, then he says we have no case. He also told me to warn you about the international consequences of illegally boarding a Russian yacht."

"To hell with that!"

"He has a point, sir."

The deliberate formality of Chib's warning wasn't lost on him. He may be reacting on gut instinct, but she was trying to make sure the investigation played out by the book. Worse case, if Garrick was right, any major error in due process now could compromise damning evidence and cause a mistrial.

Garrick felt utterly hopeless.

He took a breath to calm himself. "What do you suggest, Chib?"

"Harry is surveilling the situation. Unless he sees just cause..."

"Mark Cross. Get him talking. We need verification he left the case with Quentin Morgan."

"That won't be enough."

"No. But it will be *something*."

"I'll do that myself."

That was the last thing he heard as he pulled the wire on his hands-free earphones to move it away from his face. Once again, the phone slipped down between the console and the seat. This time the headphones pulled free, and he heard the phone slide under his chair. He didn't need the satnav now, and he'd have to stop to retrieve it. For now, time was of the essence. A new rain downpour did little to help the situation.

With no other plan in mind, Garrick continued to the marina. Even at speed, triggering every speed camera on the M20, it took another hour before he neared the harbour. He turned the siren off and unplugged the blue light, tossing it into the passenger footwell.

As he parked in the lot, he could see the super-yacht's outline picked out in low light against the cloudy night sky. He pulled his phone from under the seat and realised nobody had called him. That wasn't a surprise, the battery was dead. Leaving the satnav on had killed it.

He stepped out into the rain and wondered how he was going to find DC Lord. Assuming he was still here. He walked to the edge of the dock and was dismayed to find a metal security gate was closed, preventing access without the correct code entered on the keypad. Spikes around the outer side of the gate discourage any attempt to climb around it.

"Oi!"

Garrick turned to see Fanta behind him.

"What are you doing here?"

"I've been trying to call you."

"Dead battery." He tapped the keypad. "Do you happen to know the code?"

"Yes." In the dim light he saw her smile. "I asked the Harbour Master. It wasn't exactly rocket science. Harry's already through, watching the boat, but has seen nothing.

He's keeping his distance as he won't stop sneezing. Anyway, I found something out, the *Perkūnas*. It's the Baltic god of thunder."

Garrick shrugged. "I know."

Fanta sagged as the wind was taken from her major reveal. "Oh, so you know about Perun?"

Garrick tried to recall the name. "Another one, I think."

"Yes. It's also a nickname for a notorious Russian Arms Dealer."

Garrick looked between the yacht and Fanta in disbelief.

"Bilol Umarov?" That explained the unusual visit from Military Intelligence.

Fanta bobbed her head uncertainly. "He's certainly a suspect, but Perun's identity is still a mystery. But from what I can tell, there is a hot trade in illegal artefacts used to buy weapons." There was a tremor of concern in her voice. She lowered it to a whisper. "What have we got ourselves into?"

Garrick fixed his gaze on the silhouette of the super-yacht.

"Quentin Morgan is on that ship. I'm betting everything that he took the case with him, maybe hoping to exchange it for Liam Brady's release. And all of this got the Flanagans killed."

"What can we do? It's not as if we can walk up the gang-plank and ask if they'll let us on."

Garrick looked between the boat and his young DC.

"Why not?"

FANTA LIU STOMPED on the bottom of the gangplank to make it rattle and yelled up again.

"Hello!?" She resisted the urge to shout '*ahoy*', as she suspected it was something people only ever said in cartoons.

The young captain appeared on the *Perkūnas'* deck, backlit by a spotlight.

"Yes?"

"Hi!" Fanta waved and smiled. "I was hoping you could help. My boat's over there." She jerked her thumb towards the line of moored pleasure yachts that were a fraction of the size as the monster in front of her. "My power's out and I can't get hold of the Harbour Master." Luckily all the boats were dark and berthed for the winter. She was acutely aware of her lack of nautical knowledge so tried to keep the chit-chat general. "And I'm sleeping in it tonight." She added, hoping to garner some sympathy from the stone-faced captain.

Just several yards away, Garrick could just hear Fanta, but the captain's replies were too low to make out. He just hoped DC Liu could keep up the pretence as he clung to one of the hawsers fastening the yacht to the dock. The rope was so thick he could barely wrap his hands around it. It was slick from the rain too, but the ridges were deep enough for him to dig the edge of his shoe's soles in to stop him sliding down.

From the darkness of the dock, it had seemed like a good idea. Fanta could distract the security while he shimmied up. Harry Lord would wait, concealed in the darkness, ready to provide backup.

The reality was very different. Garrick was in pain to begin with, so hauling his overweight body up a sharply inclined wet rope was taking its toll on every muscle that wasn't numb, pulled, or damaged. Rain lashed his face and got into his eyes. One slip and he'd break his neck.

He moved closer to the hawsehole at the top of the keel through which the rope ran through. From below, it looked like a simple manoeuvre to clamber up and over the gunwale and onto the deck. But now the rope was running out, Garrick realised that he'd have to stretch almost his whole-body length to reach the rail from the top of the rope, which meant his feet would have to take his entire weight. He drew himself as close to the hawsehole as possible, so close that he could peer through to the dark deck. There was no sign of movement.

There were also no sounds from Fanta.

He carefully twisted his head to see what had happened, but he was too close to the hull, and the gangplank was hidden by the ship's graceful curves. At least it also offered him some cover from prying eyes.

His grip tightened on the rope as he psyched himself up for the last part of the climb. Was he committing breaking and entering, or was this an act of piracy? He wasn't sure, but he was certain it wasn't technically legal.

He was suddenly swamped by a wave of doubt. Was he really doing the right thing? Or had fatigue and multiple blows to the head driven him to recklessness? Either way, going back down would mostly involve a nasty fall. The only way was up. He mentally counted down.

Five... His thighs burned as he increased the pressure his feet exerted on the rope.

Four... His bandaged wrist throbbed as he held on tight. He needed his right hand to haul himself up, which meant his injured one would be the only limb holding him to the rope.

Three... When did Wendy say the baby scan had been rescheduled? Was it tomorrow? It couldn't have been today as she would have called...

Two... This wasn't going to work. He was going to fall and break his neck. A quick death he hoped...

One.

28

It was a moment in which time stopped.

Garrick couldn't feel anything in his left arm. He didn't know if he was holding onto the rope or not. His thighs ached as he pressed his feet together, while at the same time launching himself upwards. His right arm stretched out, Superman style, his fingers probing for the lip of the gunwale.

His left cheek painfully scraped against the hull. He was too close and hadn't factored in the hull's obtuse angle. At the same time his feet slipped, leaving him hanging from his damaged arm.

By some miracle, his probing hand clamped around the rail. He instinctively gripped it with every ounce of strength and felt his body swing out into space as rain pelted him from the side. The dock was thirty feet below him and he didn't have any strength left.

He couldn't recall how, but the next thing he remembered was somehow kicking a leg over the rail, while simultaneously pulling himself up with both hands. His numb arm seeming to still have its uses after all.

Then he fell several feet the other side, onto the hard wooden deck with the breath knocked out of him.

He couldn't move and waited for the scuffle of feet as Umarov's security team intercepted him. When they didn't come, Garrick rolled onto his back and sat up. He pushed with his legs to shuffle against the bulkhead so that he could recover. Luckily, he was at the prow, in an area pooled in darkness. It offered some cover, but he was sure a boat of this sophistication would have night vision cameras and various anti-piracy measures in place. Perhaps they didn't think they'd have to use them in England.

"This was a moronic idea," he muttered to himself.

Resting for as long as he dared, Garrick rubbed some feelings back into his left arm and clambered to his feet. As an experiment he tried to ball his left hand into a fist, but with limited success. He steadied himself as a wave of dizziness swept over him.

The sliding door he'd passed through when he'd met Umarov was a few metres away. Further along the deck, he could see a spotlight on the top of the gangplank, but there was no sign of the captain. He wondered if Fanta had successfully lured her away.

He'd got this far, now it was time to see it through.

Half-crouching, he made it to the cabin door and leaned against it, gently pressing his ear against the cold fibreglass. At first, he couldn't hear anything. Then a faint hum arose. He couldn't tell if it was muffled voices, or reverberations through the hull.

Garrick put his hand on the door handle and readied

himself to slide it open. He didn't have much of a plan from that point. He'd have to rely on his natural bluster.

Then came the sharp thump of a gunshot.

Garrick froze.

The door suddenly slid open in front of him. A squat black suited man with hair shorn to his scalp, was opening it. He looked at Garrick in surprise. Behind him, a body lay on the floor, blood pooling from underneath.

Garrick's hand was still on the door handle. He used his body weight to haul it back closed. He only had seconds to make his next move. One his life depended on. He should run – but that's what the security guard would expect.

Garrick held his ground as the door slid back open and the guard ran out. Straight into Garrick's fist. The man's nose crumpled with an audible snap. He staggered back into the room, straight into display plinth bolted to the floor. But the glass display case wasn't. He lost his balance and crashed through it, dislodging the chunk of stone with a delicately carved war chariot etch into it. It broke in two under his weight as he fell, cracking his head. He lay unconscious as Garrick took in the room.

Quentin Morgan was in the middle of the room, crouching over the opened silver flight case. Umarov was at the far side, looking at Garrick in surprise. He had something in his hand. Liam Brady was sprawled face down on floor, blood pumping from beneath him, and from the vivid red bullet exit hole above his kidney.

"POLICE!" Garrick yelled. "You're surrounded!"

"Don't be foolish, Mister Policeman," the Russian growled.

Umarov had one hand raised in a gesture to stop Garrick,

in the other he held a pistol, the barrel pointed towards the floor.

"Put the gun down!" Garrick sounded a thousand times more confident than he felt. He was completely unarmed. He didn't even have a stick to defend himself. What sort of idiot was he? He was wondering if he had some sort of suppressed death wish.

"You're not thinking straight," Umarov warned him. "This is not what it seems."

"I'll give you to the count of five!" Garrick barked – instantly regretting the hollow threat. What was he supposed to do after he reached one?

Quentin still hadn't moved, the bloody fool. Garrick willed the curator to use common sense and flee to safety, after all that's who he was trying to protect.

"There's no way out of this, Umarov. Even the Intelligence services know."

"Huh! There are two words combined that make little sense!"

"Five!" Garrick barked with conviction. He was a better actor than he imagined as the Russian was suddenly rattled. He raised the pistol.

Garrick threw himself at Quentin to protect him, launching himself into the air as the curator tried to stand, anticipating Garrick's move.

That's when Garrick saw the gun in Quentin Morgan's hand.

Too late, Garrick cannoned into him and both men tumbled against the heavy flight case. In a few seconds of clarity, Garrick saw the foam-lined case had five small machine guns neatly packed inside. There was enough space for another four layers

Quentin gasped as he took Garrick's full weight. The curator kept the element of surprise; only seconds earlier Garrick had thought he was saving the man. Now the end of the unfolded machine gun stock in the Englishman's hand struck Garrick's temple, causing him to roll off the man.

On his back, Quentin shuffled backwards and aimed the business end of the weapon at Garrick.

"NO!" It was Umarov.

Quentin hesitated – buying Garrick enough time to kick the barrel aside. The rapid dull thump of automatic gunfire sounded as bullets arced across the room, shattering two more display cases, punching holes in the prow-facing panoramic windows, and chewing up a section of the ceiling, taking several lights out. There was no precision, Quentin's finger had awkwardly caught the trigger. He stopped firing and quickly stood.

A feminine shriek from behind him made the curator spin around.

Fanta emerged through an internal door, clutching a small fire extinguisher which she thrust at Quentin's head. He sidestepped, and it grazed his ear before smashing into his collarbone with a sickening crunch of breaking bone.

"You stupid bitch!" he grunted.

Garrick tried to stand, a difficult task as he swayed uneasily.

Quentin twisted to the side – blocking Fanta's next blow with the machine gun's stock. Metal clanged against metal, and the fire extinguisher was jolted from her hand. Wincing in pain, Quentin put his arm around Fanta's neck and crushed hard. He was much taller than her, and his effort lifted Fanta off her feet. If she hadn't broken his collar bone, then he would've had the strength to choke the life from her.

Quentin slipped the gun barrel under her chin, not an easy task considering the weapon's length.

With a snarl, he backed through the door Fanta had come through, using her as a shield. Garrick froze, unsure what to do. Then Quentin and Fanta were gone.

Garrick noticed Umarov leaning against the bulkhead, clutching his side. A stray bullet had caught him. His pistol lay at his feet. Garrick was rusty on his firearms but recognised the shape as a Glock. It had been some years since he had attended a voluntary firearms training with seasoned Authorised Firearms Officers. He'd used a Glock then, so at least had the confidence to locate the safety catch. In pain, the Russian kicked the gun over to Garrick and nodded towards the door.

"He'll kill her," he wheezed.

Garrick snatched up the gun and gave chase. He prayed that Harry Lord had heard the gunshots and was doing something about it.

29

T he corridor lights were dimmed. Large port side windows looked out across the dark harbour, while three closed doors were evenly spaced on the opposite wall. The thick carpet beneath Garrick's feet felt like walking on sponge. There was no sign of Quentin Morgan or DC Fanta Liu.

Garrick held the Glock with both hands, the barrel pointing the way. He wasn't sure if this was correct stance, or something he had assimilated from watching one-to-many movies.

He listened but heard no sign of movement. He doubted Quentin would have cornered himself in one of the side rooms. Unless they had access across the yacht, to the gangplank. He was sure Quentin intended to leave the ship the first chance he got.

Then he remembered the chopper parked on the rear pad. Could Quentin fly? Until a few minutes ago, he had thought the bumbling curator was a victim tangled up in black market antiquities – not an international arms dealer.

As far as he knew, Quentin could fly out of here. He quickened his pace down the corridor. The carpet muffled his steps, but his foe had the same advantage.

A sliding door ahead was partially open. Garrick paused behind it, listening for movement. There was a faint clanking, possibly feet walking on metal. Keeping the Glock level with one trembling hand, he slowly slid the door fully open. Beyond was a wide deck that overlooked the bow. There were a few yachts moored on the far side of the harbour, and the lights of buildings beyond. Garrick's mental map suggested the helipad was above him. Metal steps to his left, led up to the deck above.

Pushing his body flat against the bulkhead he took a deep breath... then poked his head around the steps to get a better look. Nobody shot at him. He could see the open sky beyond the deck above and rain dripped onto his face.

He carefully walked up the exterior staircase, keeping the Glock ready. His mind was racing. Even if Harry Lord had heard the shots and called for backup, the Specialised Firearms Officers wouldn't be here for at least thirty minutes at best, and the only weapon Harry had was foul language.

At the top of the steps, he was facing the prow. He quickly snapped around and saw the dark blue Bell 505 Jet Ranger X parked on the helipad. He took a few cautious steps towards it, his finger brushing the pistol's trigger.

There was no sign of movement. He couldn't see anybody inside the cockpit. Then he noticed the rotors had straps at the end of the blades, securing the aircraft to the deck. It was going nowhere.

The sudden grumble of the ship's engine reverberated through the hull. Garrick spun around. Another set of rooms took up the centre deck. He trotted backwards, towards the starboard rail. It gave him enough of an angle to locate the bridge positioned another level up at the front of the boat. A light was on inside.

Quentin intended on escaping to international waters.

Garrick peered down at the marina below. He could see straight across to the car park, but saw no sign of Harry Lord, or any form of help.

He was on his own.

Near the end of the cabins, he noticed a narrow set of stairs set into an alcove that led up to the bridge. He sprinted towards them as the engine's timbre increased.

With each step, Garrick's options were ruthlessly whittled away. Additional support was now irrelevant. Time had run out for stalling tactics, and the situation was clearly beyond reasonable negotiation.

He assumed that Quentin Morgan had shot Liam Brady. But why now? Why not when he and Mark Cross had delivered the flight case to the museum? Unless they had delivered *the wrong case*. Perhaps as part of a double cross? He was starting to believe that Brady hadn't killed Kirsty Flanagan after all. But that was moot right now. He had other problems.

The last time he'd shouted a caution, he'd been shot at. With DC Liu as a hostage, the odds were stacked against Garrick.

That left just one feasible course of action. The one that DCI David Garrick always tried to circumnavigate in both his professional life and, as a sting of regret struck him from the way he'd left things with Wendy, his personal life too.

There were always too many loose ends. To many uncontrolled elements that bounced him across the oceans of fate. He'd always pretended to take control of a problem. That's how he'd ascended the police ranks, even if it was the collected effort of his teams that had made him a DCI. Wendy had even been the one to ask him out on a second date after their disastrous first encounter.

For once in his life he would have to take direct action.

The steps ran straight up to the bridge's closed door. As Garrick slowly ascended, he felt the yacht move. The hull squeaked as it pressed against the line of tyres and buoys tied to the dock to prevent damage. In the heat of the moment, it seems Quentin had forgot that the vessel was still moored in place.

Garrick reached for the door, anticipating it to be locked. Before he could touch it, the boat rocked as the hawsers pulled taut and rolled the yacht. The door rolled open a few inches.

Through the gap, Garrick could see Fanta curled up in the corner, blood trickling from a scalp wound but with a defiant look in her eyes. From her line of sight, Garrick judged Quentin was in the middle of the bridge. He could just see the tip of the machine gun pointing in Fanta's general direction.

The engine revved again, and the ship shook as it pulled at the ropes tethering it in place. The vibrations increased as the engines were pushed to the max. A loud crack split the air, followed by a splash. Garrick was thrust against the wall, and the door slid shut as the yacht's stern suddenly kicked out. The powerful thrust had ripped free the dock cleat, and part of the dock itself.

Time was up.

Garrick fired blindly two shots through the bridge door, aiming dead centre. With one hand weak, and the other numb, the Glock's recoil almost jerked the weapon from his hands. He hauled the door back open and powered inside.

Quentin was hunched over the throttle, blood flowing down his tweeds from a shoulder wound. His weight shoved the throttle to its stop, and the wheel had been turned hard to starboard. The yacht jolted forwards at an angle. The sudden movement jerked Quentin's submachine gun as he fired at Fanta.

The bullets strafed the deck inches from her feet, then up the port-side wall, shattering the window. Then Garrick was on him.

He slammed the hilt of the Glock hard into Quentin's temple. On TV he would have been knocked unconscious. In reality, the curator snorted like a bull and snapped his head back, butting Garrick in the face. His nose was already a mess, so another blow barely registered, but it was enough to get Garrick off his back.

Still leaning on the throttle, Quentin rolled onto his back and brought the machine gun in line with Garrick's head. The perfect O of the barrel filled David Garrick's vision as his brain registered the fatal threat.

With the ship's stern at an angle, the sudden acceleration ploughed the yacht forward into the dock as Quentin fired. Garrick didn't know how the bullets missed him, but somehow they did. The jolt flung both men to the floor.

The forward hawser Garrick had crawled aboard on, suddenly pulled taut pivoting the *Perkūnas* sideways at speed, like a lassoed bull. The vessel listed to port as the yacht arced in the water.

The machine gun fell from Quentin's hand and skittered across the floor. Fanta reached for the weapon–

Quentin tried to stand – just as the stern slammed into

the corner of another dock blocking its path. This one was not as flimsy as the one the *Perkūnas* had been moored to. This was solid concrete. The home of the RLNI launch station. It had three cars parked outside, and two boats raised out of the water, sitting on trestles for maintenance.

The impact threw Quentin and Fanta across the bridge. The sound of tearing steel was horrendous as the concrete punctured the hull and water rushed into the engine room. The helicopter ripped free from its tethers and was flung across the dock. It rolled end-over-end, rotors shattering and the glass canopy folding like a toy, before slamming into two parked cars.

From the floor, Garrick reached for the throttle and pulled it back, idling the engines. That didn't stop the ship from violently shuddering as it took on water. Garrick pulled himself up and turned around – as Quentin Morgan snatched the fallen Glock and shot Garrick.

Garrick felt a sharp pain as if he'd been punched the left arm. Quentin's face was twisted in rage as he prepared to fire again. He didn't have chance. Fanta swung the machine gun like a baseball bat, knocking the Glock out of his hand. With a yell of pent-up rage, she reversed the swing, crushing the gun barrel across the curator's throat. He collapsed in a heap.

"Is he dead?" gasped Garrick as Fanta dropped the weapon and ran to his side.

"We're sinking," she said urgently, her eyes scanning his body. "And you've been shot."

"I don't think–" Garrick began as the world around him suddenly spun around and he was plunged into oblivion.

30

When Garrick woke up, he was soaking wet. He blinked in surprise at the white light blinding him. He hadn't expected the afterlife to be so dazzling.

"He's conscious!" yelled a voice, and the light moved away from his eyes so he could see the round kind face of a paramedic. "Do you know your name?"

"Yes," Garrick snapped. "And I can also remember my pin number... what's going on?"

"You're lucky the bullet missed your sarcasm gland," Harry Lord quipped from his side. He had been walking with the wheeled stretcher as Garrick was being loaded into the back of an ambulance.

"Stop!" Garrick shouted, already climbing off the stretcher.

"Sir, you can't do that!" the paramedic protested.

"I assure you I can," Garrick said groggily, noticing his Barbour had been cut off, and a bandage wrapped around his left shoulder and upper arm. A red spot of blood was already seeping through. "Fanta?"

"She's the one who fished you out after your midnight swim." Garrick followed Lord's gaze to the *Perkūnas*. The luxury vessel had sunk up to a foot short of the deck. Now it was grounded, listing at a sharp thirty-degrees.

He could see Fanta, with a silver thermal blanket over her shoulders, directing officers who were bringing Umarov ashore from a rescue boat.

"I'll tell you one thing about the lifeboat service," Harry said. "They're bloody fast at responding. Especially when you crash into their house."

Garrick shot him a jaded look. "Thanks for the backup."

Harry gave him a hurt look. "I was taking care of the captain and calling these guys." He jerked a thumb at the paramedics. "Oh, and the other two security goons you *didn't* run into. You're welcome," he added sarcastically.

Garrick now noticed Harry was sporting a black eye, and his right hand was bandaged. He was sure he'd hear the details *ad nauseam* at a later date.

Fanta and two beefy uniformed officers led a cuffed Umarov towards a waiting ambulance. Garrick took a wobbling step towards them. Harry put his arms around his shoulder to stop his boss from falling.

"She's doing fine on her own, Guv," Harry said soothingly. "The best thing for you to do is get on the ambulance and stop destroying stuff." Garrick was about to argue when Harry dropped a threat. "Or I'll be forced to tell Wendy that her fella's being a prick."

In some ways, that felt worse to Garrick than staring down the barrel of a gun.

. . .

THE PROVERBIAL CLAIM that time heals all was turning out to be complete tosh, David Garrick thought. Three days had passed since the incident in the marina. He wore a crisp white cotton shirt, was shaved, and showered, and had slept deeply for almost the first day. It was a façade. Underneath, his whiplash meant moving *anything* provoked sharp pains in his joints.

His left wrist was so badly strained that he could barely move his fingers. The doctor assured him it would get better in a matter of weeks.

The bullet had passed cleanly through his left shoulder, damaging a ligament, but not much more. If Quentin Morgan's aim had been few inches wider, it would've struck his chest. At best puncturing a lung. He was only smiling because of the painkillers he was on.

Fanta was sporting stitches across her forehead from where Quentin had rifle-butted her to shut her up. But she was in good spirits, always happy to point out how she'd saved Garrick three times in one night. The first by clobbering Quentin with the fire extinguisher, then crushing the man's throat with the sub-machine gun, and finally rescuing him from the sinking yacht. Garrick snarked that the bridge had been in no danger of submersing, but he was thankful for his DC's unwavering courage.

So his wounds were painful, and his frustrations with the case still raw as the strands fell into place far too late for his liking.

Quentin Morgan was being held in a secure hospital ward, recovering from having his throat crushed. He'd been barely able to breathe, and it was a perfect excuse not to answer questions Garrick had wanted to throw at him.

On hearing about Quentin Morgan arrested, Mark Cross

was suddenly talkative, along with demands that the charges against him will be dropped if he cooperated. Even while plea-bargaining, he dropped enough details for the full picture to be drawn.

Michael and Kirsty Flanagan were archaeologists with a knack at finding the obscure. And obscure meant bountiful sales to museums and private collectors. They needed funds for their digs, and financiers needed a return on their investments. Even ancient history was a business deal.

Konstantin Volkov was a wealthy Russian oligarch with a passion for collecting antiques. While his personal history and financial success remained shrouded in mystery, none of the evidence indicated he was nothing more than an enthusiastic antiquities investor. As was Bilol Umarov. They were friendly rivals.

Except Umarov wanted more. Out of the two men, he was the poor rich kid. With his construction businesses, he was well established in the Middle East, and used to dealing in high-risk security situations. So when Volkov approached him to help provide security for the Flanagans in Syria, Bilol Umarov was happy to do so.

It was the unearthing of the Neolithic mask when things went wrong. And that was because of a man called Tony Addison. The name had dropped the investigation like a hand grenade. Addison was the connective tissue that linked everything together, and a name that only Mark Cross could provide.

Addison and Cross were old friends who had gone their separate ways in life. Addison was one of the many names on the list of people the Flanagans had worked with. Like many of the others, the police hadn't been able to get in touch with him for an interview.

Addison was an archaeologist who worked with the Flanagans on several digs, including Syria. Towards the end of the dig, Michael Flanagan was moving back and forth between Syria and the UK to ensure the funds were flowing. But Konstantin Volkov had decided not to continue financing the Syrian dig because it was going nowhere. Michael cajoled then argued with him, but no more money was forthcoming.

Addison had an alternative investor he'd worked with on many occasions: Quentin Morgan. At first, Michael Flanagan assumed the museum curator was dealing in black market antiquities. He didn't have much of a problem with that, as Quentin had agreed to pay the bills to finish the dig.

But it turned out Quentin Morgan was so much more than that. He was one of the biggest arms dealers in the western hemisphere – the illusive *Perun*, as he was known to the security services. He saw the dig in Syria as a perfect place to channel Russian made weapons. And Umarov and his private yacht, was the ideal transport.

For his part, Umarov didn't know about the weapons, he was just excited to be dipping his toe into the murky world of black-market antiquities.

Michael Flanagan didn't know about this, but when he discovered their operation was being used to ship new PPK-20 submachine guns, his conscience got the better of him. He was about to confront Quentin Morgan, but Addison pleaded with him not to. He knew what a dangerous man the arms dealer was.

What Michael didn't know was that Addison had ulterior motives. He was planning to blackmail Quentin Morgan by stealing a shipment of PPK-20s.

At the same time, the Flanagans unearthed *four* Neolithic masks. Determined that the arms dealer wouldn't benefit from all four, Michael concocted a plan to keep the other three hidden, and off the market. When he'd washed his hands of Quentin Morgan, the other three would be 'discovered', and the profits kept.

Michael sold the first mask to Quentin, as was the deal, although he managed to inflate the price thanks to Konstantin Volkov. There were two shipments being smuggled back to the UK. The undeclared masks, and sixteen PPK-20 submachine guns, with a plan for more to follow.

Addison's plan to blackmail the arms dealer involved threatening to hand over details of his arms network, which was a multi-hundred-million-dollar business, unless he was paid thirty million.

To achieve this, Addison had to quietly get his hands on both shipments. He turned to Liam Brady, who Mark Cross had once introduced him to when they both worked on the ferries. Brady was a man skilled in smuggling. It was something he had started while working on cross-channel ferries, and he'd grown pretty good at it.

While Michael Flanagan was negotiating a fee for the mask, Tony Addison was on one hand working as his business partner as a middleman, while on the other planning to swindle the arms dealer.

Even with his balls in a vice, Quentin Morgan negotiated Addison down to ten million.

The problem now was that Michael Flanagan had got wind of the scheme so, somewhere along the way, he switched the mask shipment.

Instead of the weapons, Liam Brady and Tony Addison now had the 'priceless' masks which they had no way to get rid of, and Michael Flanagan had the guns they needed. Realising that too much knowledge was a dangerous thing,

Michael didn't tell Kirsty the full picture when he set about hiding the weapons.

When Quentin Morgan found out about the double-cross, he had Michael Flanagan murdered, making it look like a road traffic accident. Tony Addison and Liam Brady went into hiding. Without the weapons, they had nothing to negotiate with and their lives were forfeit. With Michael dead, they didn't know where they were hidden.

Tony Addison once again turned to Mark Cross because he had knowledge of the Flanagan's home and security systems. It was originally Addison who'd recommended the Flanagans use Spitfire Security, and that had helped Cross get a bonus for bringing in a new client.

With Mark Cross on side, Addison and Brady had the inside knowledge of bypassing Kirsty Flanagan's security, they intended to break in to discover where Michael had hidden the weapons.

But that didn't happen as planned.

Liam Brady had no intention of splitting anything with Tony Addison. With ten million from Quentin Morgan and maybe even more from the sales of the three hidden masks, greed guided his murderous actions.

It was at this point, Tony Addison vanished off the scene. Mark Cross assumed the man was fearful for his life and wanted nothing more to do with the blackmail.

Brady and Addison had put together all the information they could find regarding where the stolen weapons were hidden. But it was soon apparent that alone, Brady was not the genius he thought he was. Without Addison, he ran into a dead end and turned to Cross for help.

Liam Brady broke into Kirsty Flanagan's house but didn't have time to search for anything because Quentin Morgan had arrived to talk to her. Brady had witnessed Quentin brutally murder Kirsty. She knew nothing of her husband's deception, other than a trail of clues he left. It was Quentin who stole Kirsty's car, hoping to make it look like that was the object of the break in, a car that still hadn't been found. The curator's DNA hadn't been on file, but now the police had a sample, it lit up Kirsty Flanagan's kitchen.

Liam Brady had watched Garrick and the others search the house. He'd followed them to the colliery and enlisted Mark Cross's help to retrieve the weapons before Umarov's men, acting on behalf of Quentin Morgan, could do so.

Quentin Morgan had used Umarov as his strong arm. The Russian was keen to impress Quentin, and had even bought the man's yacht to curry favour with the man. So he had no qualms planting the trackers on the police. Only from the way he behaved with Garrick showed the Russian was regretting his decision working with the infamous *Perun*. Illegal weapons were a step too far from illegal antiquities.

The Russian was still in critical condition in hospital.

Mark Cross recounted how Brady had persuaded him to accompany him to see Quentin and hand over several weapons in return for a million dollars. The remaining cash would be paid when the rest of the weapons were handed over, along with the masks for good measure.

The morning Garrick had turned up at Mark Cross's house, Cross had left to purchase some shovels to recover the masks that Addison and Brady had buried. However, Garrick had unwittingly led Umarov's men to Liam Brady, and they kidnapped him.

Garrick looked at the new timeline his team had constructed on the evidence wall. Despite the multiple players, it was a sad straightforward tale of greed and blackmail that had left a trail of bodies. Kirsty Flanagan was the only innocent one amongst them all.

It was a successful end to the case. Well, almost. Superintendent Malcolm Reynolds wasn't pleased about *something*, but it wasn't something he could articulate when he summoned Garrick to his office.

"One has the feeling things could've been resolved with less... faff." Reynolds made a circular motion with his hand.

"It's a shame we didn't have your deductive skills in the incident room. Then we could've gone home last week." After the last few days, Garrick was in no mood to hide his animosity. Whether or not Reynolds had picked it up was another matter.

"And the destruction at the marina is quite intolerable. The dock, the RNLI office, and the salvage alone."

"Shocking."

Malcolm Reynolds pressed his fingers against his desk to pick at invisible dust motes.

"With all the fiscal scrutiny on us... questions will be asked. And it appears every time they're asked, your name comes up."

Garrick gave him a thin smile. "Sir, that's most kind of you. But I'm sure I'm not the only detective on the force who keeps getting successful results."

Reynolds gave him a cold stare. "Results and costs are two very different things."

"Are you suggesting that there is a financial limit to solving crime?"

Reynolds slowly leaned forward in his seat and put his elbows on the table as he clasped his hands together.

"I'm suggesting that the two are connected." He paused but wouldn't meet Garrick's eyes. "And there is the matter of you shooting a suspect and punching a security guard in the face."

Garrick shrugged, what could he say?

"And DC Liu's violent assault on Mr Morgan. Not to mention what DC Lord did to two private security guards." He shuddered. "One man may lose a testicle..."

Now Garrick was feeling angry. For whatever reason, his Super was nitpicking protocol. He wondered if it was a reprisal because of Ms Jackson's influence from above to cut him some slack. However, Garrick didn't think there was anything to be gained from showing his anger.

"I can vouch for them both. Lives were at stake. If anything, their actions were minimal at best."

Reynold closed his eyes and rubbed the bridge of his nose.

"Yes, yes. But that's for others to assess. I'm just telling you how the IPOC may see things."

Garrick tried not to react. The mention of the Independent Office for Police Conduct was unusual given the circumstances. Wielding the IPOC as a threat, rather than try to protect his staff spoke volumes of the grudge Reynolds seemed to have against him.

His Super gave a weary sigh. "And the press attention..."

The sinking of a Russian Oligarch's super-yacht had drawn international press attention. The rumours about Umarov being linked to smuggling operations quickly followed. Garrick had avoided all contact with the press, including Molly Meyers. His Super had taken the full brunt and was clearly unused to such attention.

Reynolds pulled himself together. "Anyway, while the accountants do their thing, I am asking you to take gardening leave. Just a few weeks once you hand everything over to the

CPS. From the look of you, it would be the perfect time to recover. Put your feet up."

Garrick didn't have a reply to hand. One thing was certain, it had answered a key question for him about what he should do regarding Molly Meyers' offer to accompany her to the United States.

31

L oose ends feature in almost every complicated case. They're usually tucked away in the hope that the accused's defence team doesn't stumble over them and try to use them to unravel the case.

In the murders of Kirsty and Michael Flanagan and Liam Brady, he felt confident that there was little wriggle room for misinterpretation. That still left Tony Addison missing, which was one loose end.

The missing Neolithic masks were another.

Once Konstantin Volkov had learned about the three extra masks, any polite sympathy he'd been expressing for either Quentin Morgan or Bilol Umarov vaporised. The cachet, and cash value of the find would more than cover his investment. The problem he had was Addison and Brady were the only two who knew where they were buried, and any clues were in police evidence and Garrick had no intention of letting the man see the files.

There was a lot of data processing involved in wrapping cases up. It was more time consuming than the actual investigation which involved plenty of staring into space. In the free time they had, Garrick ensured his team went home in time, and he put Chib back on sick leave to recover, or more accurately, rearrange her wedding.

Garrick made more of an effort to take Wendy out most nights for meals, the cinema (where he fell asleep, which was unfortunate as the movie was her choice), and even bowling, which he hadn't done for years and was surprised just how much he enjoyed it. And that was with Sonia joining them too. As usual, her conversation was sparse but at least she didn't pry into his personal life.

In their moments of downtown, he and Fanta turned to WhatsApp to trade theories about where Addison and Brady could have buried the treasure. Addison could have fled the country by now and even taken the masks with him, but something told Garrick it was still worth pushing.

Michael Flanagan had left a series of clues for his wife to decipher if anything should happen to him. Garrick couldn't think of a reason the selfish Tony Addison would leave any clues behind. He was the sort of bloke who took secrets to his grave. Family had been interviewed. Members of the digs he'd worked on, anybody who could shed any light on his movements. All they had confirmed was that he was estranged from his family and was a loner.

Garrick had been glancing at a map the tech team had put together showing the mobile phone movements of Tony Addison. It was the last thing he could think of to locate the man. There was a distinct lack of personal calls made, and any contact between the phone and a cell tower had stopped two days before the bloodstained shovel had been found. Clearly, Liam's blood on the shovel was an accident and his autopsy revealed a nasty wound to the stomach which he'd had stitched up in hospital. Garrick guessed that Tony Addison had inflicted it. Had the two men argued? Had Addison left the country at that point?

The grim reality was slowly taking hold, one that Garrick was quickly leaning towards. Addison was dead. Presumably killed by Liam Brady.

One Sunday evening, Garrick as at his kitchen table while Wendy sat on the living room couch, half-watching a soap she'd recorded while shouting through to remind him of dates and times for something or other. They'd spent breakfast discussing if they should move or not, now that the money from Garrick's old house had come through. He'd never seen so many zeroes on his bank account and he wasn't in any hurry to alter that. He thought ridding himself of the bad memories attached to the house would be a weight off his shoulders, but he felt little change.

Attempting to rekindle his old interests, he'd tried to get back into cleaning up a fossil he'd found on the beach last year. His hobby had slipped him by since he'd moved in with Wendy. Staring at the dark brown stone, with the faint black lines of an ancient creature embedded within, he just couldn't summon the enthusiasm.

He didn't want to work, but he couldn't stop looking at his phone as he reviewed the hundreds of emails associated with the Flanagan case. He'd been thinking about Tony Addison all night.

He looked at the mobile phone data they'd received regarding Liam Brady. He was never off his phone. The last contact with a cell tower was outside Mark Cross's home when Garrick and Fanta had unexpectedly turned up. There was nothing after that.

On a whim, he compared times and locations with Tony

Addison's phone data. There were a number of matches which gave a strong indication both men had been together at Brady's house.

Then a match up struck him. He doubled checked the data, then dialled Fanta Liu's number.

IT TOOK until midday the following Monday for Garrick and Fanta to assemble with the canine unit and start sweeping a hillside in between the villages of Charring and Challock on the North Downs. The unit had parked on the junction of Squids Gate Lane, and corpse dogs had been deployed with handlers.

"This is a long shot," Fanta said, looking up the slope of the aptly named Charing Hill. A field gave way to forest, which was partially obscured by low cloud coverage. A dense drizzle had already soaked through the officers' clothes, but the dogs didn't seem to mind as they set off uphill, noses combing the sodden earth.

This was last location both Addison and Brady's phones had been together. After this, Addison had fallen off the face of the earth.

The hill was a popular site for hang gliders and offered sweeping views across the beautiful Kent countryside. On a clear day at least. After two hours, Garrick was losing faith in his hunch. Reynolds had surprised him by mobilising the canine unit without complaint, but Garrick suspected he was still under some pressure from above to sew everything up.

Wallowing in doubt, Garrick paid little attention when the barking of a pair of dogs drifted through the trees. Only when his radio crackled to life, did he hurry through the mist, stumbling over trailing roots, before stepping out into a clearing marked with a large boulder.

Two black labradors were excitedly pawing at the ground next to the rock. Their handlers pulled the animals back and patted them while slipping them treats.

"They've caught a whiff of something," one handler confirmed.

A forensic officer who'd spent his time sitting in the back of a van reading a comic, trudged up the slope. His white coveralls were already stained with mud as he knelt amongst the wet leaves and began carefully moving earth away with a small trowel.

With agonising slowness, he finally reached a green canvas sheet. It took another thirty-five minutes to clear a patch of dirt big enough to see where the sheet overlapped. As Fanta videoed the scene, he carefully pulled the canvas aside, revealing a corpse lying face down. Even in profile, Garrick recognised the thin features and lank black hair of Tony Addison. Maggots had already infested the soft decaying skin on his cheeks and around his eyes, and the smell was revolting, made even more so because Addison's decapitated head lay a foot away from the blood-soaked body. Garrick endured it long enough to notice something poking from beneath the torso. Partly obscured, it was the blank, plain face of a Neolithic mask.

Garrick glanced at his watch to note the time of discovery.

What he'd actually noted were several missed calls from Wendy. He'd been so distracted that he'd forgotten her ultra-sound-scan appointment had been moved to an earlier slot today. And he was going to miss it.

He barked instructions at Fanta, then turned and sprinted

down the hill as fast as he could, almost tripping several times.

He reached Maidstone hospital forty minutes later. And abandoned his car in the pay-and-display car park without a ticket. As he ran into the maternity ward, he glanced at his phone. There was a brief message from Molly Meyers confirming their US trip was on.

He double-checked with the receptionist which room Wendy was in, then barraged through without waiting for permission. Well-rehearsed apologies were on his lips when he saw Wendy lying on the couch, with the sonographer holding an ultrasound scanner to her glistening belly.

He'd expected Wendy to be angry. Instead, she was beaming with the widest smile he'd ever seen. She looked at him with wide eyes, then turned back to the screen. Garrick moved for a closer look. This time the image was easy to discern.

Wendy's fingers entwined with his own, and he felt a bubbling of emotion that formed tears in his eyes.

"Congratulations," the sonographer said.

Garrick nodded dumbly. He couldn't tear his eyes off the screen.

He didn't want to. Any doubts he'd been harbouring about fatherhood vanished. His whole future was on the screen right in front of him.

ALSO BY M.G. COLE

info@mgcole.com

or say hello on Twitter: @mgcolebooks

A MURDER OF LIES

DCI Garrick 7 - COMING SOON!

SLAUGHTER OF INNOCENTS

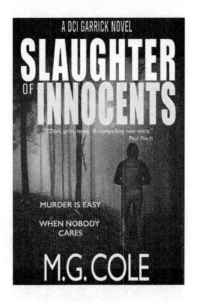

MURDER IS SKIN DEEP

DCI Garrick 2

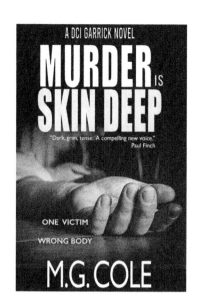

THE DEAD WILL TALK

DCI Garrick 3

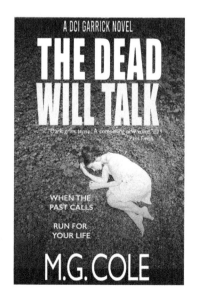

DEAD MAN'S GAME

DCI Garrick 4

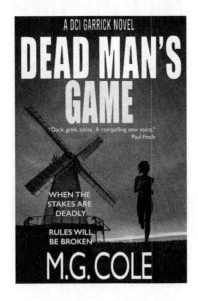

CLEANSING FIRES

DCI Garrick 5

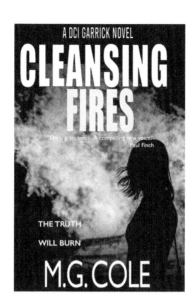

A DCI GARRICK NOVEL

CLEANSING
FIRES

"Dark, grim, tense. A compelling new voice."
Paul Finch

THE TRUTH

WILL BURN

M.G. COLE

Printed in Great Britain
by Amazon